Night Sweats, Necromancy, & Love Bites

Menopause, Magick, & Mystery

JC BLAKE

Published by Redbegga Publishing, 2021.

This is a work of fiction. Similarities to real people, places, or events are entirely coincidental.

NIGHT SWEATS, NECROMANCY, & LOVE BITES

First edition. January 12, 2021.

Written by JC BLAKE.

To all women. May you grow in power as you age and always hold magick in your hearts.

Chapter One

One thing is certain, vampires make terrible house guests. If you're a fan of vampire romance novels, or just can't get enough of 'Twilight', then you're in for a shock. You may think that it would be fun, perhaps even exciting, to share your home with a mysteriously sexy vampire version of Robert Pattinson or Brad Pitt, or maybe you really go weak at the knees for Gary Oldman's version and would love to exchange places with Winona Rider, but the reality is something else—entirely! Don't get me wrong, I'm not talking Nosferatu or Salem's Lot horrifying - there's nothing particularly unattractive about vampires, well, not in general - but they are vain, selfish, and have some horrible habits, particularly when it comes to using the bathroom! Sorry to burst that little bubble ladies, but my patience runs thin with a man who has had countless centuries to get his 'aim' right and still can't manage to 'be sweet and wipe the seat'!

The vampire my aunts invited to stay for what remained of the summer caused me grief before he even got to the house, but it wasn't until the local shops ran out of garlic that trouble really came home to Haligern Cottage.

Two days after they announced that we were to have a house guest, and five before the grand opening of *Haligern Cottage Apothecary*, I travelled to Whitby, East Yorkshire, to collect Count Vladimir Dracul aka Vlad the Impaler! I can't pretend that I wasn't terrified. A thick lock of my hair had turned white on the news and despite my aunts insisting it was a sign of my maturing magical powers, my hands trembled as I pulled into the harbour and parked my car.

My hopes of picking up the vampire without drawing attention to myself dwindled then crashed; the place was heaving. Groups of scantily clad women, some in full Goth-girl outfits, fought for space on the path with strutting clusters of men already full of beer-fuelled bravado.

My confusion cleared as the second woman wearing a bridal veil passed my car; it was Saturday night and Whitby had obviously become a draw for boozy-last-chance-before-tying-the-knot celebrations. "Hen-night city central—just my luck!" I sighed as a voluptuous bride spilling out of her black and red Gothic corset stumbled past. She raised an open bottle of Prosecco, shouted something indecipherable, then took a swig. A pair of false vampire teeth hung at the corner of her mouth then dropped to the kerb. It was only just twilight, but she had obviously started drinking earlier in the day.

When two men sauntered past in black tuxedos, sporting vampire teeth, slicked back hair, and smeared white foundation, I realised that Vlad, however peculiar he looked, wouldn't stand out as an oddity.

I scanned the harbour. Vlad's ship should have docked earlier in the day and my instructions were to meet him quayside—after dark!

The note in Aunt Thomasin's beautiful copperplate script read, 'Count Vladimir Dracul, Demeter III, quayside, Whitby Harbour. The count has an aversion to the sun, so you are to meet him after sunset.' Beneath the instructions was a post-script; 'P.S Be sure to be home before sunrise, the coven's reputation depends upon it!'. I was well aware of how each of Vlad's visits to various covens around the globe had been immortalised in gossip and knew that my aunts were anxious that his visit to Haligern Cottage wouldn't descend into scandal as it had done when the Salem coven had invited him to stay. Invited is the wrong word, no witch invites a vampire to stay, rather a request for accommodation is sent to a particular coven in full expectation of acceptance. Vlad, I had been reminded countless times over the past two days, was a man with great influence, who could act as protector in a crisis and, given the problems we had experienced over the past weeks – the theft of Aunt Loveday's grimoire and the abuse of its powers by the Blackwood clan – he was an ally to be courted.

The low but humming odour of garlic wafted from my fingers as I re-folded the note and placed it in my pocket. My aunts had assured me that vampires didn't bite witches, but the terror I held towards Vlad, fuelled by countless horror films watched as a teenager, wouldn't abate, and I had rubbed my neck with garlic just in the spot where his teeth would sink into my jugular should he feel in need of a snack!

Several boats were moored along the quayside, but all appeared to be working fishing boats. On one a man was repairing an oblong crabbing pot and a bright light shone on the deck illuminating him as though centre stage. The other boats were devoid of people.

Twilight gave way to the night, and although the quayside was well lit by crisp white light from the overhead streetlights, much sat in shadow. However, I had come prepared and shone torchlight along the side of each boat. None of the boats close to the steps was the Demeter III. Further along the quayside, at least one hundred feet from the others, and beyond the reach of the streetlights, sat one more boat. It had to be Vlad's.

I dry swallowed, instinctively rubbed my neck, and walked to the boat. The noise of my shoes tacking along the concrete walkway grew louder with each step. Twenty feet from the boat, adjacent to the last streetlight, I slowed to a stop and shivered. The boat rocked against the quayside as waves surged. The wind was picking up and the late summer air had the warmth suggestive of a coming thunderstorm. The fisherman on his boat continued to repair the nets and I took comfort from his presence despite the distance.

'Vampires have no interest in witches, you're perfectly safe' had been Aunt Loveday's final words to me as I'd dropped my car keys for the third time. I had been scheduled to leave the cottage to make the journey to Whitby at one o'clock, but had procrastinated, putting off leaving by offering to help Aunt Beatrice with the huge pot of herbs she was preparing on the stove, and then making numerous excuses as to why the time wasn't right: waiting for my phone to charge, checking the oil and tyre pressure on the car, another cup of tea, another visit to the bathroom. My stomach churned as I tried to convince myself that I could rise to the challenge of being a taxi service for a real-life supernatural being whilst every cell in my body wanted to go back to bed and bury my head beneath the duvet. 'We have a natural immunity to them,' she had said with an optimistic smile.

'A natural immunity?'

'Yes, so even if he does bite-'

'Which he won't!' Aunt Euphemia added with certainty.

'Of course—which he won't.' Aunt Loveday nodded to emphasise her point. 'But even if he does bite, his vampire virus will just wither and die in your blood. You would not become a vampire yourself,' she added for clarity.

'But he could still ... harm me, though?'

'No!'

'What about Long Lizzy Cruickshank?' Aunt Thomasin had quipped.

'Ah, yes. Long Lizzy. But that was a completely different situation. Lizzy betrayed him, she got what she deserved.'

'I'm not sure being torn into a thousand pieces could be construed as 'what she deserved' Loveday!'

'Perhaps it was a little over the top, but Vlad has a violent history. He certainly earned his nickname.'

'Impaler ...' I had said weakly.

'Yes, he was bloodthirsty in his younger days.'

'True, but that was before he became a vampire.'

'He's mellowed.'

'As long as you don't cross him, you're safe.'

'Or unless you're a wife!' Aunt Beatrice laughed. 'Then you have to watch your head!' She cackled at her joke. Vlad had beheaded one wife when she insisted on calling him 'Vlad the Impala' although the jury was still out on whether that had been a mispronunciation given that the woman had been either South African or Australian.

I stood and stared at the ship, then, inching closer, shone my torch along its hull. 'Demeter III' was painted in bright red lettering along its port side. Far sleeker than the fishing boats, it had none of the paraphernalia of a working boat and instead resembled a small yacht. However, no lights shone from its port-holes and there was no one on deck.

I cleared my throat and, in a small, hoarse voice called, "Count ... It's Liv Erikson, I've come to pick you up."

A wave surged and the boat rose, lurched towards me, then thumped against the tyres roped along the quayside. Startled, I jumped backwards only to bump into something solid.

Hot breath wafted on my cheek. "I am here ... Livitha Erikson." The voice was deep and accented with Slavic undertones.

Vlad's face brushed against mine as he leaned in over my shoulder.

I screamed.

He chuckled.

Instinct forced me to take a step, but a strong arm slipped around my waist and then I was pivoted to face the vampire.

Chapter Two

The Count twirled me round with expertise and held me as though we were dancing a tango, one arm around my back as he stared into my eyes. "Good even-ink beautiful Livitha." Already mesmerised, I could only stare back as he drew my hand to his mouth. I squeaked as brilliant white and pointed fangs brushed against the delicate skin on the back of my hand. For one terrified moment I imagined him opening his mouth and sinking them into my wrist. Instead, surprisingly warm lips pressed down gently upon my fingers.

The Count only vaguely resembled the vampire I had imagined him to be. In my darker moments he had become a terrifying Nosferatu type monster complete with hunched back, yellowing fangs and talons, and a hideously ugly face. Compared to that nightmare, the Count was almost normal, but there was no doubting he was far from ordinary.

Standing at least six foot tall, he was muscular without being beefy. Dark hair was cut short but not slicked back as per the stereotype. His nose was aquiline, his cheekbones high, and extralong dark lashes ringed startlingly blue eyes. Cleanshaven, his chin, which had a shadow of stubble, carried a central dimple. If you can imagine a cross between a middle-aged John Travolta and Henry Cavill then you have Vladimir Dracul aka Count Dracula.

I gasped at the touch of his lips on my skin and felt the heat in my cheeks rise as he unashamedly scanned me from head to toe.

Debonaire in dark belted slacks and perfectly pressed white linen shirt, he said, "Ah, Livitha, son of Soren Erikson, I am delighted to make your acquaintance." He sighed as he spoke then said, "You drive the automobile? Yes?"

My mind, already thinking of a way to politely correct his mistake, struggled to respond to this sudden change of topic.

"Yes! Thank you! Yes, I do drive. I've parked up there." I jabbed a finger at the road.

"You are strong?"

"I wasn't quite sure where this line of questioning was going, but replied, "I think so ..."

"You look strong."

My cheeks burned. "Yes ..." I faltered. "I guess I'm strong." To Vlad, I was a workhorse! I was suddenly aware of my body and every pound of unwanted, tenacious, fat. "But I'm his daughter, not his son," I added in a weak voice that carried no conviction.

For the merest second Vlad held my eyes then said, "Ah, good. Then we go." With that he turned to face the steps and with a click of his fingers said, "My luggage is on the ship. Igor will assist you."

On cue, a man stepped from the shadows between two stacked piles of crabbing pots. Startled, I managed to stifle a squeak. No one had said anything about a companion. Unlike the Count, Igor was short and stocky and looked to be at least seventy years old. He grunted as he shuffled forward then jabbed a pointed finger at the boat and gestured for me to follow him. As the count waited beneath the streetlight, I followed Igor to the boat and retrieved the Count's luggage. There were two suitcases, a vanity case, and a holdall. When I struggled to lift either of the suitcases, Igor thrust the vanity case at me with a grunt that failed to hide his irritation. Loaded with the holdall, and the suitcases, he shuffled from the boat and made slow progress to the Count waiting beneath the streetlight. Like the suitcases, the vanity case seemed to be made of lead and I was relieved when it was safely stored in the boot of my car. Slightly breathless with effort, I grasped the lid of the boot ready to close it when the clack of hurried footsteps was followed by, "Yoohoo! Vlad!"

From my position behind the lifted boot, I heard the count sigh in response to the woman's call.

High heels tacked with quick staccato beats. "He's here! I found him." Shrieks of excitement erupted and, as I lowered the boot lid, three young women dressed in elaborate Gothic style complete with bridal veils, high-heeled black boots, fishnet stockings, and overspilling lacy corsets were headed straight for us. The count had obviously made an impact on the women and they tottered at full pelt across the road, waving and calling like a pack of demented superfans.

Already irked by his dismissive attitude, I said, "You've been making friends, then!"

"Yes," he replied without humour. "I am sorry, Livitha Erikson, son of Soren Erikson, but I have some unfinished business to attend to. You will wait, yes?" Without waiting for my reply, he moved at lightning speed and had redirected the women to the town within seconds. I watched, jaw slack, my back still hurting from heaving the leaden case over the lip of my boot, as the Count steered the women down a side street.

"Count! ... Vlad!" The group disappeared and I stared at the empty space in dumb surprise. "He can't do that!"

Igor grunted, mumbled something unintelligible, clambered into the front seat of the car, and closed his eyes. I gestured to Igor to wind the window down. He shrugged. I rapped on the glass and shouted, "Igor! He can't do that! We have to get him back."

Igor shrugged again. "He come back soon." His voice was muffled through the glass.

I pulled open the door. "So, you *can* understand me!"

"Of course I understand," he replied.

"Then go tell him, he can't do that. Those women—he can't ... Listen! Go and get him back. Tell him to come back!"

"I tell him nothing."

"But ..." Images of the count melded with scenes from the horror movies of my youth; swooning maidens, entranced by the vampire, succumbed to his charms and their fate, their necks pierced, their blood drained, their bodies left in a heap on the side of the road! Haligern's reputation would be ruined! "You have to stop him."

"He only enjoys. He has party with ladies of the night."

"I don't think they are *that* kind of lady! They just kind of ... look like they are. And what do you mean 'party!'" I stared at the empty road.

"He come back soon. You no worry."

But I do worry! I opened the passenger door. "We've got to get him back to Haligern before sunrise."

Igor merely grunted and pulled at the door. "He come back when he come back."

"How long will he be?"

Igor shrugged his shoulders. "The master is his own master," he replied with enigmatic indifference, then leant back against the seat and closed his eyes.

"Sure, but how long?" I checked my watch. It was a quarter to ten. I relaxed a little; even if Vlad were gone for a few hours, there was plenty of time before sunrise. Annoyed and more than surprised that Vlad had abandoned us, I decided against sitting beside Igor, who was now snoring loudly, and made my way to the town in the hope of finding a quiet bar that served coffee. I had no idea how to handle the Count and had to trust that Igor was right, and that he would return soon.

I had only ever visited Whitby on brief trips with Pascal and never in the evenings, so decided to take a walk around the town, find a quiet café and buy a drink, preferably coffee. I found one easily and ordered an espresso then sat on a pavement table that looked out over the harbour and up to the famous abbey ruins on the hill.

My thoughts turned to Pascal. On our trips, Pascal and I would share a bag of chips then wander down the promenade, looking in the windows admiring the artisanal crafts and wondering at the unusual curiosities many of the shops displayed. On our first visit, only a year after our marriage, I had made the mistake of offering a chip to a seagull. This had turned out to be an enormous mistake and we had been harassed by the birds – which are alarmingly large and have dangerously sharp beaks – to the point where we had to escape by running into a local shop. The shop had been filled with antique and vintage jewellery and specialised in selling local jet, a black stone unique to the area. One piece, a ring with a large oblong stone set in silver filigree, had appealed to me, and Pascal had insisted on buying it—partly to placate the shop owner who realised we were using his shop as a refuge. I had chosen to wear the ring on the day I collected the Count and considered it with a pang of regret as I sipped the espresso. When had it all begun to go wrong? Had it been my fault? Was I not a good enough wife? *Stop being so maudlin! It went wrong the moment he jumped into bed with another woman. You were a good wife, attentive and supportive. It's not your fault he couldn't keep it in his trousers!* I switched off the inner critical voice and the moping, self-pitying one, rubbed a thumb over the stone's smooth face, and returned my thoughts to Vladimir Dracul and his disappearance with a gaggle of drunken Goth girls.

Nearly an hour had passed by the time I returned to my car and Vlad was waiting with impatience on the back seat. Igor remained asleep in the front. Vlad rolled the window down upon my approach.

"So ... we go now?"

"Yes," I said noting the irritation in his tone, "we go now." I bit back my instinctive response to say sorry. Vlad had been the one who had abandoned me without a backward glance, and I hadn't been gone that long. I also bit back the question I was yearning to ask—what exactly had he done with those women, or rather, done *to* those women?

With questions churning in my mind, along with horror movie clips on repeat, I started the engine with a palpitating heart and checked Vlad in the rear-view mirror for signs of spattered blood. Of course, there was no reflection of the

Count and, with hairs rising on the back of my neck, I reversed from the parking space and began the journey back to Haligern.

Chapter Three

T en minutes after leaving the harbour, we joined the dual carriageway eastbound towards Haligern. Blue lights flashed from the dark road ahead and a convoy of emergency vehicles, three police cars and two ambulances, sped past on the opposite side of the carriageway, sirens blaring. I gripped the steering wheel and turned to look back at Vlad. He was following the convoy, craning his neck to watch as they sped towards Whitby.

"Must be an accident," he said with little interest then returned to face the front.

I remained silent and focused on the road ahead, my mind whirling. Had he bitten those women? Had he drained them of blood and left them to die in the street? I gasped as a thought struck me. Whitby would become the epicentre of the undead!

"Livitha, son of ... sorry! Daughter of Soren Erikson, are you feeling well?"

My head pounded, my mind tripping over the scenarios—refusing to believe he would, refusing to believe he wouldn't. "I have a tension headache," I replied. This wasn't a lie; I did have a headache. "Driving at night strains my eyes." This was also true, but not what had given me a pounding headache that matched the thudding of my heart. "And, please, it's just Liv."

"Justliv, son of-"

"No. Liv. It's short for Livitha and, in England, we don't use the 'son of' patronymic lineage ... thing, it's kind of old fashioned."

Vlad chuckled. "I am an old-fashioned kind of man, Livitha. I have lived many years. For centuries I have walked in the shadows."

Igor snorted then muttered under his breath. I had no idea what the jumble of words meant.

"Ignore him, Livitha, daugh- ... Sorry, Liv. Ignore Igor's warped sense of humour—he is a fool, a dunce, a dimwit. Please do not take offence; he has the charisma and social grace of a parsnip!"

Igor grumbled, but didn't rise to his own defence and I became certain that Vlad's stay with us was going to be a trial. So far, I didn't like him very much and wondered if Igor wasn't the only one who had the social grace of a parsnip. Vlad was handsome, enigmatic, and obviously charismatic to some, but I was discovering a side to him that was far from genial and it was becoming obvious just why he had had so many wives, even making allowance for the length of time he had been alive, or rather undead.

"No offence taken, Count. I wasn't aware he'd make a joke." It was a weak response. Part of me wanted to rise up and defend Igor against the Count's rudeness, but the other part of me knew that would cause great offence and the one thing I didn't want to do – with the details of his wife's death still fresh in my mind – was cause the Count any kind of offence. Instead, I forced a smile, gave a rundown of how long our journey would take and mentioned how happy my aunts were to have him as a guest at Haligern. Placated, the Count sat back in his seat.

"I think I shall sleep, Livitha."

"That's a good idea," I agreed as the Count closed his eyes.

An hour passed in silence with both the Count and Igor asleep, or perhaps feigning sleep, but I was glad of the peace and quiet and used the time to think about the opening of my aunts' shop, *Haligern Cottage Apothecary*.

Unbeknownst to me, Aunt Beatrice had long harboured a desire to open a shop in the village, specifically to sell the products my aunts made. For years they had supplied home-made herbal remedies, sometimes with a secret magical touch, to the villagers. Their lotions and potions treated all manner of ailments from teenage acne to arthritic joints. They were particularly popular with older ladies for a face cream that worked miracles on ageing skin. They also offered more 'magical' items such as love potions (watered down!) and cleansing sticks. Their soap was as good, and I thought better, than any artisanal soap you could buy in the shops and used flowers and herbs from Haligern's gardens and milk from our cantankerous, but plentiful goat, Old Mawde. Uncle Raif had promised to make some of his besom brooms for sale too although he often seemed to tire easily these days so I hoped he wouldn't overdo it in an effort to please my aunts.

I had been surprised and flattered when they informed me that I was to be the shop's manager and was doing my best to make it a success. A grand open evening was planned and although the date was quickly looming, there was still much to do. I was prepared to work as many hours as I had to, to get everything ready for that evening. However, although I was pleased that my aunts had considered me for the role and was genuinely excited to be a part of their new enterprise, I harboured another desire; to become a private detective. It was really only a fantasy I played with, but I knew if I had the opportunity to set up my own business, I would jump at it. I knew nothing of setting up a private detective business of course, hadn't done any costings, didn't have a business plan, or even know if there was a demand, but searching for clues about the murder of my husband's mistress had sparked my interest.

The journey seemed endless, but the end was in sight when I was finally able to take the junction off the main carriageway. Brightly lit roads became winding country lanes lit only by the car's headlights. A heavy fog had sunk to hover above the road in thick patches and I slowed as visibility became limited. My already strained eyes began to burn with tiredness. However, despite the fatigue making my head throb, my thoughts were racing and chaotic and I was in the process of imagining Whitby's Goth Weekend overrun with actual vampires when the car's engine failed.

The car came to a rolling stop. The orange light on the fuel gauge shone like a beacon from the dashboard, the dial pointing to empty. I groaned as I realised my mistake. I had valeted the car, making sure every surface was dust-free and polished, and the upholstery vacuumed and freshened. I had checked the oil and the windscreen wash. I had even washed and waxed the bodywork. But I had forgotten the most vital thing—to fill the tank with petrol!

"Is there a problem ... Liv?"

"Yes ... we're out of petrol."

Chapter Four

I stared dumbly at the orange light signalling the emptiness of the fuel tank. Igor grunted then huffed, crossing his arms to further showcase his annoyance and Vlad remained silent in the back seat. Claustrophobia descended on me like the heavy fog that surrounded us. I fumbled with the doorhandle as I told them I would call for help and explained that I would get a better signal outside. A fine haze of moisture coated my face as I stepped out of the car and took a deep breath to ease the tension across my chest. Worse than having to sit with the men, was the thought of letting my aunts down. Vlad was sure to let them know exactly how incompetent I was.

I took out my mobile phone, began to dial Haligern, then pressed cancel. I couldn't call my aunts for help. For one thing there was no petrol stored at the house and it was after midnight. Somehow, I had to sort this out myself. I toyed with the idea of flying, after all, if the legend were true, Vlad had the power to turn himself into a bat and fly through the night sky. I could find a suitable broom-like stick and take Igor as a passenger. However, for a start, it would be rude of me to suggest that Vlad take flight and make his own way to Haligern, and for another, I had only experienced broom-flight once and that had resulted in me tumbling out of the sky when a monstrous imp had attacked me. I shuddered at the memory but at least that problem had been dealt with as soon as Arthur, Aunt Loveday's ancient and powerful grimoire, had returned home. Coming on top of her increasing worry about Uncle Raif's health, the spell to rid the Black Woods of the beasts Tobias Blackwood had conjured, had taken its toll—another reason I didn't want to disturb my aunts.

Scrolling through my contact list there were only two names on it that I could turn to: Garrett Blackwood and John Cotta. I scrolled between both names, unsure which to call. In the car Igor had turned on the interior lights and now sat picking his nose whilst the Count was watching me with a disdainful expression through eyes that had a definite red tinge. My options narrowed to one. There was only one man on the list who I could explain my peculiar passengers to, and only one that I suspected would be able to cope with the revelation of their identity. That man was Garrett Blackwood, my one-time childhood sweetheart.

Since meeting Garrett again, after a gap of more than thirty years, I realised that my feelings for him were as strong as ever, but he seemed to have no interest in asking me out. I had finally given up hope and taken up Dr. Cotta's offer of going for a coffee. He seemed keen to want to get to know me and, despite being overwhelmed by the thought that such a good-looking man could possibly be really interested in a fifty-year-old, menopausal, newly separated, frazzled frump like me, I had taken him up on his offer. Dr. John Cotta was a man of robust intellect, as well as being extremely good looking, but it was Garrett that I felt an affinity with. His family, and the curse under which it lived, were shrouded in mystery, but I suspected he was aware of magick and the dark realm just beyond ours. I wasn't certain, but I believed that he must know I came from a long line of witches and that Haligern was our coven.

There were so many questions I wanted to ask Garrett, so much that I wanted to know about his family, particularly what had been kept in Blackwood Manor's turreted room? With scored panelling and heavy shackles at each bedpost, I suspected it had something to do with the Blackwood curse. However, that would have to wait, right now I needed his help to get the Count and his familiar back to Haligern Cottage.

The phone rang and I coughed to clear my throat just as he answered. Spluttering followed as a coughing fit struck.

"Liv?"

I heaved for breath.

"Liv? ... What is this?"

"Just a minute." My plea came out as a rasp.

"What are you playing at, Liv?"

"Please!"

I held the phone away, forced several coughs to clear my throat, then returned it to my ear. The line was dead.

"Damn!"

I called again and was answered by an unwelcoming 'Hello!'

The sense of wanting the ground to swallow me up, which seemed to accompany every interaction I had with Garrett, attacked me again.

"Sorry!" I blurted. "I had a coughing fit."

Silence, then. "Right ... I thought ... well, never mind what I thought. Is there a problem? It's two in the morning."

"Two! Sorry! I'm so sorry for waking you at this hour, Garrett. I wouldn't unless ... you're the only one I could call."

"Liv, what is it?" His voice was filled with concern now. "Are you alright? Where are you?"

"I've run out of petrol. I think I'm about thirty miles away from Haligern. We took the junction about five miles back."

"We?"

"Yes, me and ..." I caught Vlad's eyes. "A visitor. A friend of my aunts. I'm just on my way back from collecting him."

"Okay, never mind about all of that. So, what can I do to help?"

"Well, I was hoping you could ... and I know it's an imposition, and I'm so sorry ... but I was hoping you could bring me some petrol or give me a lift to a petrol station. I'd walk, but ... well it's rude to ask a guest to walk and ... and it's a bit far and I have no idea where the closest petrol station is."

"Are you in the car?"

"No, I'm just next to it."

"Okay." His tone was officious—in control. "Return to your vehicle. Switch the hazard lights on. Keep your mobile at hand. I'll be there as soon as I can."

With those instructions, the line went dead, and I returned to the car.

Inside, the air was now fuggy, and the windows misted. I explained that my friend was on his way and that we should remain in the car until he arrived. Igor grunted. The Count remained silent though offered me an unimpressed nod then followed it with, "We wait for your friend, Livitha. I have time to wait." He grew silent, his face morose and he turned to look through the window to the hedgerow illuminated by the flashing orange light. "I have lived many centuries ... time is something I have much of."

Igor covered a derisive snort with a faked sneeze.

The count narrowed his eyes and pursed his lips but continued to stare out of the window.

"Yes, well, we do have *some* time," I said, although I was becoming worried. Sunrise was only a few hours away. My understanding of vampire biology was that sunlight was fatal and that his cadaverous flesh would bubble and then melt should its rays land upon him. Informed by movies, I imagined the sun rising and light sparkling on a beam until it hit the Count. He would begin to writhe then melt horrifically in the back seat of my car until there was nothing left but a puddle of slime in the footwell. Alternatively, the sun would strike, and he would burst into flames, leaving a conical pile of ash on my back seat—a stain that no amount of fabric cleaner would remove! Neither scenario was acceptable. I checked my watch. Ten minutes had passed in uncomfortable silence and I was about to suggest a game of 'I spy' when Vlad swung the car door open and stated that he was going to 'explore the wilderness of your country' before disappearing into the shadows.

It was impossible to see in the dark, and the haze of fog also muffled sound, but a distinct flapping of wings was followed by a chitter as the Count disappeared. Igor remained in the front seat, still far too interested in the contents of his nostrils, but at least had the good grace to turn away from me whilst he picked! My stomach churned and after ten minutes of sitting in silence with the vampire's familiar I left the car. Orange hazard lights pulsed in the mist. In the distance an owl hooted and something screeched, possibly a fox or a deer and I wondered if the Count only drank human blood, then became concerned as to exactly where he was going to get a regular supply of haemoglobin during his stay with us. My aunts had mentioned nothing about what he would eat during his stay and I was unsure whether he supped exclusively on blood, or had a wider diet—raw meat, or even offal? Maybe the movies and books had it wrong? Perhaps he'd sit to table at Haligern and join us for Irish stew and dumplings followed by one of Aunt Beatrice's delicious bramble and apple crumbles?

"Livitha!"

Hot breath brushed my cheek in a déjà vu from earlier in the evening as the Count hung over my shoulder. Deep in thought, I was oblivious to his return, and yelped as he spoke my name.

"Ah, Livitha, I startled you. I apologise." Despite the words, his tone was insincere, and I got the impression he found my reaction amusing.

"No, I'm fine. It's okay," I stumbled as I regained my composure. "My fault ... I was away with the fairies."

"Excuse me? I don't understand. Where have you been? I haven't seen any ... fairies around here."

I noticed him shudder as he said 'fairies'. His mask of calculated indifference also twitched.

"There are no fairies here."

The barest hint of relief passed over his face.

"It's just a saying. I was deep in thought so didn't notice your return."

"Ahh! Yes, I see, although I have the stealth of a cat, Livitha. After so many years of walking in the shadows – for a split second his gaze flitted to Igor in the car – I have become an expert at arriving in silence. It gives me the element of surprise ..." Here he raised his eyebrows and his eyes flickered red as he smiled to reveal bone-white fangs. In that moment it struck me that he was no different to Lucifer, my acerbic familiar. Both were arrogant, crept about at night hunting down their prey, had a sharp edge to their tongues, and were prone to complaining.

Discovering that my childhood pet was my familiar, could talk, had some magical powers of its own, and an irascible temperament, had taken some getting used to, but I was beginning to learn how to manage him. However, I doubted whether the Count would be as easily mollified as Lucifer was with a saucer of port and slice of salmon.

A few words of sympathy about his suffering in the shadows elicited a smile and I was about to ask the Count about his aversion to fairies when the noise of an engine broke into the night and headlamps illuminated the fog.

Chapter Five

The haze of fog grew bright and then a car appeared through the mist as though being birthed. It slowed to a stop less than ten feet away.

"This is your friend? Yes?"

"I'm not sure, but I think so," I said. It was impossible to see who was in the car but as I took a step forward, the door opened, and Garret's voice called from behind the light.

"Liv?"

"Garrett! Yes, it's me."

The door slammed and then footsteps crunched over gravel but still Garrett didn't appear. Almost a minute passed as Garrett retrieved emergency triangles from his boot and placed the flashing orange signs twenty feet from the rear of his vehicle.

"Liv!"

"Garrett!"

"You took some finding. This is the second to last turn off before the one for Haligern."

My error only compounded my sense of failure. "I'm sorry!" I said with genuine remorse. "That must have been a pain! How did you find me?"

"Well ... let's just say I have contacts who helped me out." Through the flashing orange haze, I could see that he was distracted. He frowned and peered at my hair. "Liv!" he said with a look of bewilderment. "What happened? I mean ... sorry! Did you do that on purpose? I mean, have you been to the hairdressers?"

Suddenly self-conscious, I touched the thick streak of white hair. "Don't you like it?"

"I ... yes, it reminds me of something ... someone."

"Frankenstein," the Count declared and stepped out of the shadows.

Startled, Garrett flinched, shock registering on his face as he stared at the Count now towering over my shoulder. "Frankenstein?" His bewilderment turned to a frown. "What exactly are you saying?"

The tension was immediate.

"Frankenstein," the Count repeated. "She looks like the bride of Frankenstein. You have seen the film, yes?"

"Oh!" Garrett managed a smile as he realised the reference was a compliment and not an insult. He glanced at my hair. "Yes, I think you're right. She does!"

"I have seen it many times. Valerie Hobson was superb. Ah! The bride—such a beauty." The Count gave a long-suffering sigh. "Always it is the brides that cause the trouble."

"I suppose-"

"You are a married man?"

"I ... no, well, once, but not anymore."

"Then you are one of us. Always they disappoint. Take Frankenstein's bride for an example. Poor monstrous, misunderstood man! When his bride, she wakes, and realises what Frankenstein really is, she has the hysterics and runs." An enormous sigh full of regret followed. "It is the human condition, I think, always to be horrified by what we truly are. You agree?"

Listening to the Count philosophise on the human condition in the thickening fog with Garrett was surreal.

"Well ... I suppose." Garrett's bewilderment only seemed to deepen, and he stood, jerry can in hand, staring at the Count like a rabbit caught in headlights.

"I am so sorry!" I said in an overly loud voice in a clumsy attempt to break the awkward moment. "Garrett let me introduce you to ..." Introducing the Count should have been easy, but how on earth could I introduce him as Vlad Dracul *the* Count Dracula? "This is-"

The Count came to my rescue. "Vlad Tepes," he said using his alternative name. I only hoped that Garrett wasn't aware it meant 'impaler' in Vlad's native tongue. "I am here to see your beautiful country." The Count stepped forward to shake Garrett's hand. "Ignore my ramblings. I must thank you for coming to our assistance."

"Garrett's a DCI," I added.

The Count offered a large pale hand with surprisingly chunky fingers. Garrett remained bemused, as though he were trying to fathom some difficulty, but took the Count's hand and shook it. "DCI Garrett, I thank you."

"No problem," Garett returned, then held up the jerry can, and offered me a stiff smile. "I stopped off at the petrol station."

"Thanks!" I was overly enthusiastic. "You're a life saver."

The passenger door opened, and Igor shuffled to the front of the car. Unable to hide his surprise, Garrett stared at the hunch-backed elderly man for several seconds longer than was polite. Igor grunted then mumbled something in his native tongue. To my surprise, Garrett replied in that language.

Igor chuckled and flashed a jubilant smile at the Count. The Count huffed.

"Ignore his warped sense of humour, Garrett Blackwood-"

"Shall we fill up the tank, Garrett?" I interrupted. "My aunts will be worried sick if we don't get back by daylight." I emphasised 'daylight' and was relieved when the count took the hint.

"Ah yes, we must return before the day's light."

Igor mumbled again then chuckled. Garrett threw him a bewildered glance then his eyes flitted to the Count.

"Yes, before my aunts wake. They're always up by daylight and if we're not back by the time they get up, I'll be in trouble!" I said this with forced humour. I was desperate not to have to explain quite who the Count and Igor were to Garrett, but it was obvious he thought the whole situation peculiar. I was also deeply concerned at the Count's reaction to Garrett should he discover Vlad was a vampire; the whole situation could go horribly wrong and I was regretting asking Garrett to help. Although my aunts had insisted that the Count had made a solemn oath to behave during his stay with us, I was unsure whether he had already broken his promise and bitten the three Goth-girls back at Whitby. Garrett could be his next victim!

However, as Garrett removed the petrol cap and began to decant the petrol into my fuel tank, the Count and Igor returned to the car. Alone with Garrett I was lost for words. Nothing I wanted to say was appropriate in that moment. I felt like a teenager facing a neglectful boyfriend, desperate to ask if we were going to see each other again, desperate not to be rejected, desperate not to seem desperate.

The last of the fuel glugged from the jerry can.

"All done," Garrett said as he replaced the lid.

"I can't thank you enough," I said, holding back the flood of words; *you said you would call ...*

"You're about five miles from the crossroads. Take a right and you'll be on the road to Haligern."

"Thanks," I replied.

"It's easy to lose your bearings in the fog."

"It is."

"Erm ... Liv. Can you do me a favour?"

"... Yes, I would think so."

"Call me when you get back. I'd like to know you're safe." He took my hand again, stroking the fingers that had been mauled by the Witchfinder. He glanced at the car. The inhabitants were hidden behind the misted windows. "Liv ..."

"Yes."

"I don't know what's going on ..." He gave another sideways glance to the car, "but ... we need to talk."

"Oh ... okay."

"Good."

"Yes ... good."

"Right." He released my hands. I felt an immediate pang of loss. "Hop in and start the engine."

I followed his instructions and turned the key in the ignition. The engine started without a problem and I wound the window down. "It's great now, thanks," I said.

"Good!" He tapped the car's roof and bent down to look inside. "Good to meet you, Vlad."

The Count gave a regal nod from the back seat.

Garrett turned his attention to Igor. "And you too, erm ..."

"Igor," the Count offered. "My travelling companion."

"Good to meet you, Igor."

Igor mumbled a reply and the twitch of a smile appeared at the corner of his mouth.

"Liv," he said, "Don't forget to call."

"I won't," I promised.

With that he returned to his car and disappeared behind the light shining from the headlights.

"So, Livitha," the Count said as I secured my seatbelt, "you are popular with the men here?"

"I'm not sure about that ..."

"I know these things," he stated, then leant forward. "I have lived a long time, Livitha, and I know when a man loves a woman. When you have suffered for love as I have suffered, then you know."

Igor made an indistinct noise.

"Love certainly makes you suffer," I agreed.

Igor chuntered.

"Hah!" The Count said with enthusiasm. "I knew it. You suffer as I do, Livitha. This man, this Garrett Blackwood, he is your soulmate."

"Oh ... Garrett's just an old friend," I said as I watched his car's backlights disappear into the fog.

"No, he is more! I sensed it in the beat of his heart. And in yours. I am old. I know these things."

"I'm not sure I'd go so far as to say soul-"

"Your soulmate, Livitha, just as my Mina is mine." He gave a theatrical sigh. "Just as I suffer, so do you! Forever will I walk in the shadows searching for my Mina. Forever will I suffer until I find her. But YOU! You have your soulmate here. Do not lose him! Do not become like me! Lonely and forever searching the dark realms for the woman I love! Or man, in your case! I am cursed, Livitha! Cursed to walk through the shadows for eternity."

Igor shook his head. "Pah!"

"Ignore him, Livitha. He does not understand the suffering we must endure because of our tender hearts!"

Igor mumbled.

"Ignore Igor, Livitha, daughter of Soren Erikson. He has a peculiar humour. He is a dimwit. A dunce. He has the social grace-."

Of a parsnip. I released the handbrake and began to accelerate. "Let's go home."

Chapter Six

The remainder of the journey was uneventful, and I pulled into Haligern Cottage's driveway an hour before sunrise, victorious, if not a little exhausted. Light shone from the kitchen window and the front door opened as the engine died.

Four figures pushed out onto the steps as Igor opened the car door for the Count to disembark.

The Count was received with great ceremony, with Aunt Beatrice giving a nervous curtsey as he mounted the steps. Vlad returned their welcome with perfect grace, but it wasn't until he had been shown to his sleeping quarters in the cellar that I breathed a sigh of relief.

Before you imagine a dank, dark room for the count to inhabit during his stay, let me put your mind at rest. Our cellar was certainly dark, but it was kept clean and was relatively damp free. There were no clusters of fungi blooming in the corners, no moss growing in the mortar, or rats creeping in the rafters, or mice scurrying over the doorframe. The entire space had been swept, washed, and cobwebbed and it now contained the belongings the Count had sent prior to his arrival. These items consisted of a heavy antique armchair with an elaborately carved frame with seat and back upholstered in a fraying tapestry fabric, threadbare in places. A large Persian rug also showed signs of wear. Inlaid with brass in a design that looked like it could be the Count's crest, was a narrow chest of dark wood. There were also several elaborately moulded brass candelabra along with candles. The largest item though was a lacquered and lidded box into which we had poured the sacks of earth that had accompanied it. The earth had been overlaid with a sheet of impermeable membrane and topped with a large rug of animal pelts. A blanket had also been placed within the box, but this was of a modern fleece material printed with an image of a majestic artic wolf baying at a full moon beneath a star-speckled midnight sky. The box and its blankets was the Count's daybed.

During the evenings and nights, when he would be awake, he had the use of two connected rooms along the corridor from me, one with a large and comfortable bed, the other furnished with a small sofa and television. Igor had a bedroom close to the Count's and had been invited to use the sitting room downstairs when not on call for his master.

My aunts had gone to enormous trouble to make the Count welcome and, so far, he seemed appreciative. After half an hour of talking, and polite replies to my Aunts' questioning regarding his journey and health, he retired to his 'day room' with a courteous smile without having mentioned me running out of petrol or taking the wrong junction. We gathered in the kitchen to gossip.

"Well, he is so much more handsome than I imagined!" gushed Aunt Thomasin.

"He certainly is good looking."

"He reminds me of someone," said Aunt Euphemia. "Someone modern."

"Well, I think he looks a bit like the actor who plays super-man or John Travolta."

"Yes! It's that dimple on his chin."

"And so polite!"

I restrained the urge to give my opinion on the Count and instead agreed that he was attractive and had been polite. In desperate need of caffeine, I placed the kettle on the stove, then remembered I was supposed to call Garrett to let him know we had arrived safely. With the kitchen full of chatter and sure that Garrett would ask me awkward questions about the Count, I chickened-out of calling and sent a text message instead. I desperately wanted to talk to Garrett, but I wasn't in the right frame of mind at that moment. I placed my mobile back in my pocket then noticed the spattering of soot falling from the chimney.

"Fairies!" I whispered as the soot sprinkled on the dusty hearth.

My aunts were in the full flow of conversation, deep in discussion about the Count's good looks and the gossip surrounding his ex-wives.

"I'm not surprised he has so many," I quipped with my eyes still on the chimney breast. My comment went unnoticed. "Aunt Loveday!" I squeaked as a tiny, soot-speckled creature zipped from the chimney. It rose in a flash to the ceiling then swooped back down and sat beside Lucifer's empty saucer. Chittering followed. "Aunt Beatrice!"

"Yes, Liv?"

"I thought the fairies had gone!"

"They have," she replied with certainty.

"Then why is there one in the kitchen?"

The chatter among the women stopped.

"In the kitchen! Where?"

"Right there," I said jabbing a finger at the tiny creature. It sat with its knees to its chest, its cloud of white hair catching the morning light and glowing gold.

"Oh!" Aunt Thomasin said as she caught sight of it beside the saucer. "I think it wants something to eat."

"I knew it!" I said with exasperation. "We should never have fed them." During the infestation, the only way to quelle the riotous little monsters as they searched the house for their lost baby had been to feed them a breakfast of my aunt's stinky homemade cheese mixed with a few drops of elixir to make a soporific paste.

"We can't risk another infestation, sisters. Not with the Count here. I've heard he absolutely detests fairies, and that the feeling is mutual!"

If the Count's aversion to fairies was anything like mine, then he was in for a difficult stay at Haligern Cottage if the little monsters returned. Life would become unbearable once more!

"Loveday, I thought that you were going to consult Arthur for a fumigation spell."

"Isn't there a magical equivalent of an exterminator?" I asked.

"Tsk! You talk about them as though they are vermin."

"Shh!"

All eyes returned to the tiny guest beside the saucer of milk. It chittered then began to rise, hovering by beating its tiny wings.

"They are beautiful, though," Aunt Thomasin sighed.

"Indeed, but it can't stay."

"Feed it and perhaps it will leave."

"No!" I yelped.

"Stay calm, Livitha, dear."

"If you feed it, we'll never get rid of it."

"Then what do you suggest?"

"Encourage it to go home."

"Home is the shop, dear."

It had come to light that the fairies had travelled back to Haligern from the old sweet shop that my aunts had bought to transform into their apothecary shop, the shop where I was going to be manager. I patted my hair, half expecting the other side to have grown white. There was going to be no escape from the little creatures.

The fairy rose to eye level and it was then I recognised it as the mother of the fairy larvae I had rescued from Blackwood Manor. On its back was a papoose complete with fairy child. "Cild Aelfen," I whispered as I became mesmerised by the tiny, and exceptionally beautiful fairy. The head of her child rose just above the papoose. She flew towards me and, despite the increasing sense of panic, I stood my ground and let her come close. Turning to show me her baby, she chittered. I responded with appreciative cooing noises and realised that, at least in that moment, she was harmless. "I guess we're stuck with them," I sighed, "but there is no way they can live here. I just cannot cope with them sneaking into my bedroom and messing with my stuff whilst I sleep."

"We can banish them from the house, now that we have Arthur."

"I'm surprised you haven't done that already, Loveday," Aunt Thomasin said. "Remiss of you, dear."

"I was so pre-occupied with looking after Raif, and then there were all the arrangements for the Count ..."

"Understandable."

"Absolutely."

"It's not your fault at all."

"How long do you think they've lived at the shop?" I asked, remembering Mrs. Driscoll's comments about seeing one there as a child.

"Well, now that I remember it, there were stories even when the queen was alive."

"She still is," I replied.

"Oh, yes, of course. I meant the old one. The sad one."

"The old one?" I scrabbled through my memory.

"Which one was it, Euphemia? Your memory is better than mine. There have been so many coming and going, I've lost track."

"Well, there was Elizabeth."

"That's the one we have now, dear."

"No, no. The other Elizabeth."

"Elizabeth the first? Are you saying there have been fairies at the shop for more than five hundred years?"

"It's very possible. Their lineage is ancient. The first ones arrived before even Loveday sailed over the sea. Isn't that right, Loveday."

"It is, but I think the queen you are referring to is Victoria, the one whose husband died young. She always wore black and became quite fat."

"Comfort eating."

"Hmm."

"Indeed."

"It doesn't do to wallow. Terrible for the figure," Aunt Thomasin said with a quick glance my way.

Suddenly aware of my less than slender shape, I pulled my jumper away from my overly generous middle.

"Yes, hmm."

"Can we get back to the issue?" I said to a background of murmured agreement about the problems of wallowing and weight gain.

"Which is?"

"The fairies." I gestured to the tiny creature still hovering between us.

"Ah yes. What were you saying about them?"

"Well, it struck me that the fairies have infest- ... lived at the shop for decades, if not centuries, and it was only our renovations that disturbed them."

"Ah, yes. Very true, Livitha."

"Absolutely."

"Well, now that all the renovations have finished, perhaps we should encourage them to take up residence there again."

"In the shop?"

"Yes."

Four pairs of sparkling, magic-filled eyes, cast their gaze on me.

"You want them at the shop?" Aunt Loveday said in surprise.

"Not really, but it's our fault that they became homeless."

"But they would live in the shop, dear. Live there. Permanently."

"Yes, that's the idea."

"But you're terrified of them."

I watched the tiny creature and its swaddled baby flutter to the ceiling. "Well, I was, and they can be a torment, and I couldn't cope with them here ... but at the shop ... I think I could cope with that."

"Ah!" Aunt Loveday smiled then placed an arm around my shoulders. "That is very fine of you, my dear. Very fine indeed."

"So, it's agreed?"

"What exactly are we agreeing to?"

"That we encourage the fairies to go home—to the shop."

"But they love my cheesy paste," Aunt Beatrice said, and disappointment flickered in her eyes.

"We can feed them at the shop," I suggested. "The whiffy cheese paste will keep them subdued whilst we have customers."

"Oh, they're far better behaved than they were, now that their child has been returned."

"Quite."

A broad smile spread across Aunt Beatrice's face. "Yes! I'd like that. I've grown rather fond of the little creatures."

The fairy landed on the huge Welsh dresser beside a cluster of glass bottles.

"You'd like that too, wouldn't you," Aunt Beatrice said addressing the creature. Its head of fluffy white hair seemed to nod and then it took off again, wings buzzing, and disappeared back up the chimney.

"Talking of the shop, now that the Count is here, we really must get organised. The opening is less than a week away!"

Chapter Seven

The next few days were tension-filled as we got used to our new guest and his nightly wakefulness. We were also busy getting ready for our grand opening which was now looming close. On the third day after I had collected Vlad from Whitby, and with him safely tucked up in bed for the day, the kitchen became a hive of activity as we continued work to re-stock our supply of produce for the shop. The village fete, where my aunts had booked a table to promote *Haligern Cottage Apothecary* had been far more successful than anyone imagined, and we had sold far more bottles of lotion and jars of salves than anticipated. The consequence was that we were now low on stock for the grand opening! And the last thing I wanted was for the newly sanded and waxed shelves to be bare.

I tied another piece of hemp around a bunch of mugwort collected during the last full moon to make a smudging stick for cleansing houses of negative energy or unwelcome spirits. A surprising number had been sold at the fete with one poor lady, her face haggard with worry, confiding in my aunts that there was something in her house. Ghost hunting and exorcisms weren't an area we were familiar with, but my aunts had passed on the number of a ghost hunting team they trusted. I wasn't interested in ghost hunting myself, but I was more than a little curious about the case. I finished by reciting a charm for cleansing over the finished smudging bundle, then tied on a label reading 'Cleansing Stick. Use thyse to cleanse your dwellinge of troublesome ghasts and spirytes' written in Aunt Thomasin's beautiful copperplate script.

"So," I said, "Mrs. Avery, the lady who wanted to buy ten smudging sticks from us at the fete, did she call the ghost hunters?"

"Funny you should ask," Aunt Euphemia replied, "Meredith telephoned whilst you were at Whitby."

"And?"

"And Mrs. Avery called her, explained about her ghastly problem, and Meredith has agreed to help."

"Ooh, do you think she'd let me join her?"

"I doubt it Livitha. Your energy wouldn't help. Encouraging spirits to leave can be a tricky business, particularly ones that are ignorant enough to stay once they have been requested to leave. They're often quite rude and disruptive."

"And vindictive, Euphemia, don't forget that."

"You're right, Beatrice! And vindictive. Quite honestly, I'd stay as far away as possible from the situation as you can. We can always ask Meredith over for elevenses once she has closed the case?"

"I'd like that," I replied. Since my brush with investigating who really killed my husband's mistress, the sleuthing bug kept chewing at me and I was keen to meet Meredith, and her business partner, Peter, and ask them all about their business. Running the apothecary was going to be fun, but I had decided that I'd also like to do some private detective work on the side—if I could. "She sounds like an interesting woman."

"Oh, she is. I know you'll love her!"

The conversation turned to the salves, potions, and soaps that were being prepared for the apothecary shop. Thankfully, there were enough bars of soap left to stock the shelves, at least for the first week or so, but new batches were in the process of being created, cured, and dried and this morning the kitchen carried a heady aroma of calendula and orange with an undertone of rich honey.

Aunt Beatrice flitted between a large pot on the stove and another hung from brackets above the open fire. The room was already hot, and I opened a window to let in some fresh air and then opened the door. Sunlight spilled across the tiled floor and I yelped as Benny, Aunt Thomasin's midnight black raven swooped through the open doorway. He landed on her shoulder and rubbed his head against her cheek. Of all the familiars, Benny was the most respectful and although he might peck at Bess, Aunt Beatrice's whippet familiar, and Lucifer, my feline familiar, he was never insulting. In fact, he was usually affectionate, helpful, and always protective. Aunts Loveday and Euphemia were 'between' familiars although Loveday had begun to mention finding a new one soon. Bess bounded in behind him and was suddenly underfoot. Lucifer followed behind, slinking between my ankles before wandering over to his saucer then fixing me with piercing green eyes. "Liv!"

Bess brushed against my leg as she capered around the room.

"Calm down, Bess!"

"Liv!"

"Just a minute Lucifer!" I said as I tied off a piece of hemp on another smudging stick, this one of sage with a central stem of lavender.

"Liv!"

Benny took flight and flew out of the window but not before swooping down and pecking Bess' rump. The whippet yelped, dived under the table, scrabbled over my feet, then disappeared out of the door.

"Liv!"

"Lucifer, what is it?"

"If I have to ask ..."

He fixed me with accusing eyes and knocked a paw against his saucer. The last time I had been busy and forgotten to give Lucifer his breakfast had resulted in a temper tantrum and then a curse. I didn't want a repeat and knew that placating my acerbic familiar would be the best way of being able to get on with preparations. "I've saved you a lovely piece of roast pork, Lou." I threw him a smile. His accusing eyes remained fixed on mine. "And there's some cream in the fridge that-" He shook his head. "Some port on the sideboard?" A white incisor appeared at the side of his mouth—his version of a triumphant smile. With a small sigh of resignation, I left my work and prepared his breakfast, chopping the roast pork and pouring a saucer full of port as he slinked around my ankles. Lucifer purred in ecstasy as he snaffled the pork and lapped at the port. It was enough, I hoped, to buy me some peace whilst I worked.

As Lucifer licked the last of the port from his saucer Mrs. Driscoll arrived.

"Tsk! That cat'll be getting gout!" She said catching sight of Lucifer as he wobbled away from the saucer. Her comment was an accusation, and she raised her brows whilst fixing her eyes on me. "I've never seen the like! A cat drinking port and before nine o'clock too!"

Lucifer glared at her then shot an angry look at me. I returned his stare with a grimace and a shrug of my shoulders but knew from his glare he expected to be defended. "Well, it's five o'clock somewhere," I quipped, unsure whether she was more offended that the cat had been given alcohol or was drinking during the day.

"Tut! He's an odd one, that's for certain," she said with a smile. Lucifer stared at her with disdain. "But we do like old Lucifer, don't we!" Her voice was friendly, if not a little cloying. "Here puss, puss! Here puss!" She bent to pet him, tickling him under the chin and at the back of his ears. Despite her reprimand, he rewarded her by purring loudly and slinking around her legs. As soon as she had his confidence, she picked him up, placed him outside, and closed the kitchen door. "There! That's better. I don't mind pets in the house, but when I'm cleaning, I like to clear the deck and that one," she gestured to the closed kitchen door, "has a habit of getting under my feet."

"He does," I agreed, remembering the multiple times he had deliberately laid down just where she was about to dust or polish. One of his favourite tweaks was to sit in a chair he knew she would need to hoover then dig his claws into the fabric as she tried to remove him.

Lucifer yowled from the garden. I couldn't hold back a chuckle imagining him stropping off, tail held high.

The preparations continued and with Mrs. Driscoll and Aunt Euphemia out of the way doing the housework I became the witch's apprentice, collecting herbs and flowers from the garden with Aunts Beatrice and Thomasin, learning the plants' names and their properties, what tinctures and salves they would be used for, and what charms to recite as I plucked them.

By mid-morning, it was time for a break, and we all gathered in the kitchen for elevenses. With half the table already filled with bottles of lotions and jars of salves, and stacks of sweet-smelling soaps, we clustered at one end where a pot of tea sat brewing alongside a plate of biscuits.

"Well!" said Mrs. Driscoll as Aunt Loveday poured the first cup of tea. The exclamation was an announcement; she had gossip to impart.

Teapot held aloft, the table grew silent, as we waited for Mrs. Driscoll to continue. It was part of the ritual. Mrs. Driscoll always had some news to bring to the table, usually about an infidelity or faux pas.

"There's a rumour going round the village that the morgue is haunted!"

"Ooh!"

I was disappointed. I had hoped for an update about the geriatric doctor and his much younger, very married, practice manager, both of whom had disappeared several weeks ago, supposedly together.

"What are they saying?"

"Old Bill Crabtree saw something out there, among the graves, when he was out taking his dog for a walk. He said it weren't natural and his dog became so scared it pulled him over and slipped his lead. Poor old man ended laid up for days with a bad knee."

"Poor Bill!"

Aunt Beatrice reached for a jar of ointment from one of the boxes. "Give him some of this. Tell him to rub it on his knee morning and night. It'll soon come right."

Mrs. Driscoll took the jar with a smile.

"Aunt Bea!" I said. "That was meant for the shop."

"Yes, yes, dear, but Old Bill needs it now."

"Yes, but ... we won't make any money if you give it away," I complained.

"Phst! There's more to being an apothecary than making money, Livitha!"

"There is," I said tentatively, "but we're running it as a business, Aunt Bea, and you've asked me to be manager."

"I have, and you'll be a wonderful manager too."

An awkward silence fell, and I felt churlish for raising the issue; Aunt Bea was right, the shop wasn't even open, and the ointment would help Old Bill.

"Has anything else happened there, at the morgue?"

"Which morgue are we talking about?" I was unaware of any morgue apart from one at the local general hospital which was at least thirty miles from the village.

"The one at the crematorium," Mrs. Driscoll explained. "There's a funeral home there with its own ... facilities ... and a mortuary ... for the deceased." Her discomfort in discussing the details of the crematorium was obvious.

"I had no idea they did that." My experience of funeral homes was limited. None of my relatives had died during my lifetime, none that I knew of anyway, apart from my mother and father, and they had died before I could remember them.

"Yes, it makes it all easier. It's a bit gruesome though, I admit. One of Agnes' friends works there, an older girl, Mindy."

"Does she say it's haunted?"

"Agnes said she's been a bit quiet lately, and not said anything about the rumours, confidentiality I suppose, but as far as I know she enjoys working there." Mrs. Driscoll shuddered.

"She ... cleans and dresses them, does their makeup, makes them look presentable when there's an open coffin—that kind of thing."

"Perhaps we should call in Meredith and Peter?" I suggested.

"Who?"

"They're ghost hunters."

"Paranormal detectives, Liv," Aunt Loveday corrected. "And I can pass on their number to the owners if they are concerned."

"Oh, I have no idea about that. It's just gossip that's going around the village, that's all."

"So, no one else has reported anything strange?" I asked. Vlad had been with us for a few days and left the cottage each evening. He had promised not to feed on the locals, but I wasn't sure how much we could trust his word and half expected Mrs. Driscoll to report sightings of vampires.

"Well, Tammy Lebrec said she's seen something out there too. One night when she was driving home after seeing her boyfriend—he lives in the next village—lovely man, very tall with a big beard, works for the forestry commission."

"And? What did she see?"

"She's not sure. Some sort of light moving around."

I was disappointed, but also relieved. "Oh."

"But it was gone midnight, so no one should have been around at that time and it's quite secluded. Apart from Bill's cottage its half a mile to the nearest house."

"Hmm. It does seem odd," I agreed although my personal opinion was that it was a non-story.

There were murmurs of agreement and then the conversation returned to Agnes and how she was getting on at college, the difficulty of buying essentials such as garlic in the village, and other general chit-chat.

Chapter Eight

The afternoon progressed with more preparations and we continued working until supper. As the light failed, and dusk grew to dark, we ate the last of Aunt Beatrice's crumble, this time with pouring cream rather than custard.

A knocking noise came from the cellar.

"Is that the Count?" I asked.

The knocking was followed by a muffled shout.

"What's wrong with him?" I asked.

Aunt Beatrice shrugged her shoulders and continued to eat her crumble. Uncle Raif groaned then excused himself and hurried to the sitting room.

"I don't think Uncle Raif is very happy about the Count being here," I said as the key turned in the lock of the sitting room door. "Is he afraid of him?" I ventured. Unlike us, Uncle Raif, though centuries old, wasn't a witch so didn't have the immunity to the vampire virus. "Perhaps we should ask the Count to leave?" I suggested. The thought of any harm coming to my beloved Uncle was more than I could countenance.

"Now, now, don't fret, Livitha," Aunt Beatrice chided. "Uncle Raif is perfectly safe."

Once again, Aunt Beatrice was tuning into my thoughts. "I do wish you'd stop that!" I said with a touch of irritation.

"Do what?"

"Listen to my thoughts."

"I'm not!" she protested.

Aunt Loveday threw me a glance. "It's obvious to us all that you're concerned for Raif, dear. We don't need to be able to read your thoughts to know that."

"Quite," answered Aunt Beatrice.

"But Uncle Raif doesn't have the protection we do!" I insisted. "What if the Count is a danger to him?"

"There's no need to worry, Liv," Aunt Loveday said. "The Count has promised-"

"I'm not sure his promise means much," I said remembering the women at Whitby.

"Livitha! You mustn't talk like that!" Aunt Thomasin said with a glance to the doorway then whispered, "He could hear you!"

The knocking and muffled shouts repeated from beneath our feet.

"I don't think he will—at least not right now."

"Nevertheless, Livitha, we must be careful in the choice of our words. And besides, I have cast a protective spell around Raif, so he is absolutely safe around the Count."

"Then why don't you tell him that?"

"He does know."

"Then why is he so afraid?"

"He's not."

"But he practically ran to the sitting room when he heard the Count waking."

"Yes, he did," Aunt Loveday smiled. "But that's because last night he made the mistake of inviting the Count to share a glass of port and then the Count sat with him until two am. Poor

Raif was exhausted this morning. He couldn't get away; Vlad just kept talking."

"He is rather chatty," Aunt Thomasin agreed, "and does seem to have latched onto poor old Raif."

Aunt Euphemia chuckled. "I know! Poor Raif was telling me about it this morning. He's desperate not to make the same mistake again. I think he'll be going to bed early for the rest of the Count's stay with us."

"I guess he's lonely," Aunt Loveday said.

"Little wonder!" I quipped.

"He told Raif that he is waiting for someone special to come into his life. He had a terrible time with his ex-wife which is why he asked if he could come to stop with us. He told Raif he needed some 'down time.'"

"He's hoping to reunite with a woman called Mina."

The muffled shout returned.

"Do you think he's stuck?"

"Hmm, could be."

"Isn't it Igor's job to help him up from sleep?"

"Where is Igor?"

"He went into the village a while ago."

"And he hasn't returned?"

"No, but I was expecting him for supper," Aunt Beatrice gestured to the empty place laid out at the table.

The knocking became hammering.

"Do you think we should ... perhaps ... help the Count? It sounds as though he's stuck."

"I must check on Raif," Aunt Loveday said with sudden urgency.

"I've got to clear the plates." Aunt Beatrice turned to the sink.

Aunt Thomasin picked up two bowls from the table. "Me too."

"I've just remembered that Old Mawde needs some extra hay," Aunt Euphemia stepped to the back door.

I sighed. "So that means ... I have to go?"

"If you wouldn't mind, Livitha."

"That would be very helpful."

"Perfect."

Aunt Beatrice turned on the tap, Aunt Euphemia disappeared out of the back door, and Aunt Thomasin collected the used bowls and cutlery from the table whilst studiously ignoring me.

"Right!" I said, as yet another thump came from below. This time it was followed by a bellow of 'Igor!'

"Best hurry, dear," Aunt Beatrice said as she turned the tap to fill the bowl and squirted washing-up liquid into the flow of hot water. "He sounds quite distressed."

"Right!"

The entrance to the cellar was beneath the stairs and I opened the door to a waft of cold air and another bellow of 'Igor!'. It was obvious that the Count was trapped in his day bed and, torch in hand, I hurried down the steps to what had become Vlad's bedroom.

When we cleaned the room, it had a musty odour, now it was infused with the aroma of expensive men's cologne. The coffin-like box took central position, raised from the floor by trestles at either end.

"I'm just coming, Vlad!" I called as another knock came from the box.

"Igor! Where have you been?"

"It's Liv. Igor's ... out."

"Out!" the count shouted as I unhooked the first clasp that secured the box's lid. "Out! What do you mean he is out?"

I released the final clasp and slid the heavy lid to one side. The count's eyes stared back at me, red with anger. Startled, I took a step back. The Count raised a hand. "Please, do not be afraid. I am always a grouch in the morning."

"It's night."

"Yes, yes! You know what I mean. When I wake, I am the bear with the sore head."

I struggled to find something to say and came out with a pathetic, "Oh, well, don't worry about it. I'm used to it. Pascal was a bit like that too."

"Pascal, the philandering toad? Yes, I have heard of this man. It is good that he is not in your life. I would rip his heart out and throw it to my wolves." He pushed his fleecy, wolf-print blanket to one side and sat up in his box in one fluid movement, exactly like in the horror movies. I restrained a shudder.

"Well, it's kind of you to offer, but we're getting a divorce, so ..."

"Ah yes! It is something we have in common, Livitha. Both of us are unlucky in love." He held out a hand. I stared at it for a moment and he prodded it towards me. "Take it, Livitha. Help me from my bed."

"Oh! Yes." I stared for a second more at the chunky bone-white fingers with their overly long nails and then took his hand. Like his lips as they'd kissed my hand when we'd met, his hand was far warmer than I expected.

He laughed. "I am not what you expect? Huh?"

"Not quite," I agreed.

"You think I will be like the monsters in the films and television?"

"I guess," I said with an embarrassed laugh. He was absolutely right; I had expected something more frightening.

"Igor lights the candles before I rise." He gestured to the candelabra on the bureau. "Now, even he, my faithful servant, is neglecting me!" An air of resignation fell over the Count as he stood beside me. "They all neglect me, Liv! Leave me to walk alone."

"I'll light the candles for you, Vlad," I interrupted before he began to reminisce about ex-wives and his Mina. "Can I get you anything for ... breakfast? I know it's night, but would you like some toast? Or I can cook you some bacon and eggs?" I had slipped into dutiful wife mode; bacon and eggs was Pascal's preferred weekend breakfast. "What about coffee? Do you drink coffee?"

"That is most kind of you, Livitha, but I do not eat meat. I am a vegan."

I stared at him in dumb confusion; how could a blood-sucking vampire be a vegan?

"I eat nothing with a face!"

"Oh, so ... how about toast and marmalade with a cup of coffee. I make a great cup of coffee. Pascal always said so," I rambled.

"Pascal, Pascal, Pascal. Livitha, this man was disloyal to you. He does not deserve your loyalty."

"Sorry! I'm not being loyal ... I turned him into a toad, you know," I said by way of defence. "A really ugly one."

"Hah! That would have been an amusing sight, but Livitha," he said bending to me and baring his teeth, "you should have chopped off his head! It is what he deserves."

"I ... well ..."

"Never mind!" He said with a dismissive flick of his hand. "Let us go upstairs. I will join you in the kitchen after I have dressed for the night."

I returned to the kitchen whilst Vlad went upstairs to his suite of rooms. There was still no sign of Igor, but my aunts were busy in the kitchen.

"So, Vlad tells me he's a vegan."

"Yes, Vlad *is* a vegan."

"But ... how can that be?"

"He only eats plant-based products."

"Nothing with a face. That's what he said."

"Yes, he told me that too, but he's a vampire!"

"Yes, he is."

"So, how can he be a vegan when he drinks blood?"

"It's only humans he drinks from."

I was stunned.

"He doesn't touch animal products."

"Quite ethical really."

"Indeed."

"Certainly."

"Oh, I don't think it's a moral choice," said Aunt Thomasin. "Vlad was explaining it to me the other night – we were sharing a moonlit walk – and it's more to do with the blood having an ill effect on him."

"Well, what ill effect?"

"Oh, yes. Well, drinking from the dead would kill him. That's why vampires only drain a person to the point of death then let nature take its course."

"But that doesn't explain why he's a vegan."

"Makes him bilious." She patted her tummy. "Anything with animal remains, blood, flesh, and so on, gives him the jips."

"So, you're telling me that Vlad gets ... diarrhoea if he eats meat?"

"Or dairy."

"Even dairy, ooh, poor man. Imagine having to go through life without being able to eat a hot buttered crumpet."

"Or chocolate!"

"Must be hell!"

"No wonder he's always so morose."

A general murmur of agreement.

"He does pine, rather."

"I think that's because he's lonely."

"Do you think he's depressed?"

"It's that woman he's always talking about ... Mina."

"I valk through the shadows!" Aunt Thomasin cackled.

"Thomasin!" Aunt Loveday hissed with a quick glance at the doorway. "He's our guest. Please don't mock him. If he heard, it would cause great offence!"

"Yes, but he's so ..."

"I know, but really, we must be careful with the choice of our words."

Aunt Thomasin nodded. "Sorry, Loveday," she said but couldn't hide a smirk then did a silent impression of the Count as Aunt Loveday turned her back.

I snorted, a mouthful of coffee making its way to my nose.

"Thomasin! I know what you're doing," Aunt Loveday berated.

"Sorry, Loveday," Aunt Thomasin repeated without any sincerity.

"I'll get some sunflower margarine," Aunt Beatrice said with determination. "At least then he can have some of my crumble."

Chapter Nine

I woke in the night to the television blaring in the next room, the bedroom that had been adapted to Vlad's living room.

The sound of blasting guns was followed by screams and I remembered that as we sat in the kitchen, Vlad had spoken of his interest in cinema, and particularly action movies, his favourites being *Blade* and *The Dark Night*. He claimed to have watched every single vampire movie ever made and was particularly enamoured by *Interview with a Vampire* for its depiction of the hidden suffering of his people and declared that it was 'so much better than the book with all its frilly words!' His favourite, however, was Francis Ford Coppola's *Dracula* followed by *Van Helsing* in which he particularly admired the role of Kate Beckinsale. When I had challenged him about this, declaring that she was a vampire hunter, not a vampire, he had replied, 'Yes! And isn't she magnificent!' His eyes had gleamed but quickly dulled as he returned to sadness. I recognised the signs and quickly changed the subject before he became maudlin about walking in the shadows and losing 'my Mina' once more.

Guns rat-a-tatted incessantly for ten more minutes before I could tolerate the noise no more and rapped on the Count's door. When no answer came, I listened closely for any indication of movement inside, then opened the door. Curtains flapped at the open windows and, after a quick check in both rooms, presumed the Count had gone down to the kitchen for another cup of coffee, closed and locked the window, then neatened the curtains before turning the television down.

I returned to bed and quickly fell asleep only to wake to an incessant knocking. Presuming it was the Count moving about his room, I pulled the duvet over my head. The knocking continued and, increasingly annoyed and unable to sleep, I switched on my bedside light and reached for my kindle. My bedside clock read three am! The Count's nightly activities were becoming a nuisance, but with my aunts' insistence that we should avoid offending him at all costs, I determined to visit the nearby town and purchase some ear plugs in the morning. As my kindle came to life, the knocking repeated and it was with creeping realisation that the noise was coming from my window. Someone had either climbed the ivy that clung to the wall or had used a ladder.

The knocking returned, although this time it was more of an insistent tap as though someone were using a metal implement.

For one ridiculous moment, I imagined that it was Garrett, cursed and outcast, our love forbidden by prejudice, forced to climb to my window and beg that we become lovers. But he was no Romeo, and I no Juliet, and something else entirely demanded my attention.

Pulling my dressing gown on over my nightshirt, I approached the window and its heavy curtains. The tapping was accompanied by scratching and, as I peeked between the edges of the fabric, a pair of red eyes stared into mine. I flinched and stepped back from the curtains as though scalded.

Vlad's tap was followed by a muffled, "Livitha!"

Heart racing, I opened the curtains. Vlad waved then gestured for me to open the window. There was no way I was inviting him into my bedroom. Countless movies watched as a teenager had schooled me that inviting a vampire into your room was always a bad move. "Go to your own window!" I mouthed and, after gesturing for him to go to the room next door, I closed the curtains and made my way there.

As soon as his window was opened, he clambered through the gap, strode to the other side of the room, and turned to me with a dramatic swish of his cape. "It was locked!" he accused, hands on hips. Brilliant blue eyes held mine, and I was struck again with just how much he looked like a middle-aged cross between Henry Cavill and John Travolta. He was an imposing figure, and when his energy bristled, as it did in that moment, quite terrifying.

In an effort to placate him, I told the truth. "I'm, sorry!" I said, pulling my dressing gown a little tighter, particularly around the neck. "That was me."

"You locked me out!" His eyes flashed red.

I took a step back as he took a step forward. "I'm sorry!" I repeated. He moved across the floor with speed and I held my breath, but he only brushed past me to stand beside the sofa, obviously agitated. The scent of tobacco and alcohol wafted with him. "I didn't mean to. I came in here—the television was blaring. I thought you were downstairs in the kitchen."

He huffed, unclasped the chain at this throat, and threw his cape onto the sofa.

"Why don't you just use the front door?"

He huffed again then dropped himself onto the sofa. "I couldn't find the key, and anyway, I like to use the window." His voice was petulant. He sighed, tipped his head back against the cushions and closed his eyes.

"Did you go ... anywhere nice?"

"No!"

"Oh. Well, that's a shame, although I guess there's not that much to do at night around here. The nightlife never was up to much."

"That is true. It is very dull."

"Did you stay local?" Since the Count had arrived and begun his nightly excursions I had wanted to know where he went, and exactly what he got up to.

"Maybe ... I travelled far, but I found nothing of interest."

"You didn't stop for ... dinner?"

"No. I was not hungry."

It was obvious that the Count was in no mood to share details of exactly where he had been, but I had to know the truth. I pulled my dressing gown belt a little tighter. "So, Vlad, I've been meaning to ask you ... I know it's kind of personal, but ... how are you sustaining your energy?"

He threw me a confused frown. "Sustaining my energy?"

"Yes, you know, you didn't eat anything tonight and with you saying you're a vegan well, I'm a bit concerned ..."

"Ah, always the mother hen! Nothing for you to worry about, Livitha. I have much strength."

"Okay, it's just that ... well, vampires drink blood and I know that you promised you wouldn't ... do that ... whilst you're here!" I caught my breath as the words finished tumbling from my mouth.

"Hah! Always they are suspicious," he muttered and pursed his lips. "I, Vladimir Tepes, Count Dracula, have given my promise that I will cause no harm whilst I am the guest of the Haligern witches!" His eyes glowed red. "That, Livitha, daughter of Soren Erikson, will have to suffice! Now," he said and was immediately by my side. "I have had a long night. I am tired." With gentle pressure he gripped my elbow and ushered me to the door. "Tomorrow I search again."

"Oh, I see!" I said with realisation. "You went out to search for Mina!"

"Yes!"

"And I guess you didn't find her?"

"You are correct, Livitha."

The Count's eyes flitted to the window. "Igor, he is back? Yes?" He made a display of being tired, stretching his arms wide and yawning to reveal sharp and bone-white incisors. "I am very tired. I will rest then return to my bed downstairs."

As the scratching repeated, Vlad opened the door and walked me into the corridor. "I will see you in the evening, after I wake."

Back in my own room, my curiosity roused by the Count's reaction to the scratching at his window, I opened my own and peered outside. There was nothing to see and, putting the noise down to a bird that had disappeared into the surrounding and thickly growing ivy, I returned to bed and fell back to sleep until Lucifer's scratching at my bedroom door was followed by a demanding yowl.

Chapter Ten

The following morning as we set about another day of potion and lotion production, Mrs Driscoll arrived. Lucifer snaffled his final mouthful of breakfast as she bustled into the kitchen. Licking the last drop of milk from his saucer whilst eyeing her, he flicked his tail, muttered something about double-crossing deceivers, then stropped from the room before she had a chance to scoop him up and deposit him outside the kitchen door.

"Good morning, ladies!"

Her greeting was met with an enthusiastic response; we were all relieved that her spirits had picked up since the incident with Agnes. Mrs. Driscoll had been mortified that her own daughter should steal from the cottage, but once we assured her that we didn't hold her responsible and thought no worse of her for it, she calmed down and returned to her usual sunny self.

"Well!" she said as she took off her coat.

Aunt Beatrice turned from her cauldron of calendula infused liquid hung over the hearth and warming over a low fire. Aunt Thomasin looked up from her work writing out labels in her beautiful copperplate script. Aunt Loveday stopped wrapping a bar of artisanal soap dusted with complexion-clearing magick, and Aunt Euphemia righted the copper pot with its long and narrow spout that was used to add concentrated potion drop by drop to the bottles of health-giving elixirs. Mrs. Driscoll had gossip to impart and, with her audience ready, she began.

"Have you heard the news about Mrs. Acaster?"

A communal reply of, "No! Tell us."

"Well, she's had a terrible accident! They found her at the bottom of the stairs! She'd been there for days before Nancy Swift found her and she only checked because she noticed the milk hadn't been taken in."

"Days!"

"The poor woman."

"Oh! That's terrible."

"Dreadful!"

"Is she in hospital?" I didn't want to presume the worst.

"Yes, she is."

A sigh of communal relief filled the room.

"Was she badly hurt?"

"Well, Nancy said she hit her head on the way down the stairs but apart from being shaken up, a sprained wrist, and some bruising down her side, she's alright. They've got her on a drip to replace the fluids."

"I wondered why her shop was closed."

"Oh, that's not why it's closed! It's got a new owner! Sandy from the butcher's said she's seen boxes of stuff being taken inside. And that's what I needed to tell you! The new owner is making a big fuss about re-opening the shop."

"So, it's still going to sell antiques?"

"Yes, but Sandy said the rumour is they'll be selling other things too ..."

"What kind of other things?"

"Well ... things to do with the occult!"

My tension eased; although we sold the odd 'magical' item such as our smudging sticks, the apothecary shop didn't specialise in occult items.

"And ... handmade soaps and creams and lotions!"

My heart sank. "You said that the new owner was going to make a big fuss about re-opening the shop?"

"Yes, and that's the other thing I had to tell you. She's having a grand opening and there's a real buzz about it!"

I groaned. A grand opening so close to our own, particularly of a shop that may sell similar items, was bound to water down interest in our opening.

"When?"

"Tonight!"

"She can't do it tonight!" I protested. "That's just not fair. We've put so much work into getting the shop ready for tomorrow!"

"Perhaps it won't be as bad as you think, Livitha. We have loyal customers, and I'm sure they'll support us and attend."

"And don't forget we have cake!"

"I know, it's just that we've gone to such a lot of effort to get ready for our own grand opening. This other shop sounds intriguing and if there is a buzz about it's opening then people will go to that one and not ours!"

"Oh, there's a buzz about yours too!" Mrs. Driscoll wasn't convincing.

"I hope so." My answer sounded morose even to myself.

"Now, that is quite enough Livitha! You sound as though you're giving up and you haven't even begun to fight," Aunt Loveday reprimanded. "Commerce can be ruthless!"

"And you haven't even seen the shop. There may be nothing to worry about. What do you say, Mrs. Driscoll?" Aunt Thomasin asked, obviously looking for support.

"Well, it does all look rather fascinating ... I mean it's all so mysterious, people are excited to know what's behind the windows."

Aunt Thomasin sighed with resignation.

Being unable to see into the shop would only add to the intrigue! "You mean you can't see into the shop—see what she's selling?"

"No, it's all blocked out, but the display she does have looks lovely. Really fascinating."

I groaned.

"Your shop looks lovely too," she added quickly.

"And the new and improved shop is opening tonight?"

"Yes. Nine pm."

"Such late opening hours!"

"It's all arranged to create the 'buzz', I'm sure."

"Certainly."

"We're doing the same. An open evening."

"Indeed."

"I'm going," I said with determination. "Whatever she is doing, we're going to do better!"

"Good girl."

"I'm sure it won't have any impact on our own opening."

"Of course it won't."

"It will be an entirely different kind of shop, you'll see."

"I think it's invite only, tonight," Mrs. Driscoll said with an apologetic tone. "Tomorrow's the day it opens proper. You can come with me then, if you like."

"That's very kind of you, Mrs. Driscoll, but *we* open tomorrow!" Even Mrs. Driscoll was deserting us in favour of the new and intriguing shop!

Defeat began to roll over me as my phone rang. The name 'Dr. Cotta' was printed on the screen. I answered with mixed feelings, still unsure why such a good-looking and intelligent man would want to bother with me.

"Hi!" I sounded disinterested and instantly regretted my tone.

"Liv?" He sounded hurt.

"Hi, there," I said with more enthusiasm. "Sorry, I didn't mean to sound rude."

He laughed in a friendly tone. "You didn't, so stop apologising. So, I was wondering ... I enjoyed our coffee the other day ..."

"Yes, me too," I replied. It was true, I had enjoyed it. Dr. Cotta had been entertaining and seemed interested in me, my life, and my family. But there was the sticking point; it was tricky talking about my family without tripping over my words as I made huge efforts to conceal my aunts' true nature. Sworn to secrecy, I couldn't let him know that we were witches, and that Haligern Cottage was just one coven among at least a dozen others in the country.

"So, I was wondering if you'd like to come to dinner with me tonight?"

"I ..." I faltered. I had decided to visit the new shop and assess exactly what kind of threat it was to *Haligern Cottage Apothecary*. "Well, I'd love to ... but ..."

"Oh, well if you'd rather not ..."

"No! I mean, yes! I mean, I do want to go to dinner, but there's something I have to do tonight."

"Oh, that's a real shame because I was going to take you to the opening of that new shop. It's invitation only and I've got a ticket plus one, and I thought-."

Hah! "Yes! I'd love to be your plus one!"

"Oh! That's great!" I could sense the massive grin on his face and felt a little ashamed that my enthusiasm was for the ticket rather than being with him. "We can go to dinner afterwards. I've been told *The Imaginarium* in the village is good.

"Sounds perfect," I said already panicking about what I'd wear and how I'd style my hair.

"Great! I'll pick you up at eight-thirty if that's okay?"

"Sure ... great ... yes. I'll be ready."

"Bonza! See you then."

I waited for 'Call Ended' to appear on the screen then in triumph said, "I'm going!"

"That's nice, dear! Where?"

"The opening of Mrs. Acaster's new shop."

"It's called *Arcane Treasures* now," Mrs. Driscoll corrected.

"An interesting name and even more reason to go."

"Can I ask with who?"

"Dr. Cotta!" I replied unable to hold back a huge smile.

"You seem very ... happy about that, Liv?"

My aunts exchanged glances whilst Mrs. Driscoll widened her eyes. Disbelief shone there as she uttered a 'lucky you!'.

"Thanks," I replied. "He's a nice guy."

"A very nice guy," Mrs Driscoll said unable to hide her disbelief. "A real heartbreaker. There'll be a lot of jealous women in the village."

"Well, we're just friends ..."

"Hmm, well, enjoy your evening anyway." With that Mrs. Driscoll took a fresh cloth from beneath the sink and began to wipe down the windowsill.

Unlike Mrs. Driscoll, my aunts didn't seem overly impressed with my plans.

"So, you're going with Dr. Cotta to the opening?"

"Yes!" I said unable to hold back the triumphant smile. "Mrs. Driscoll was right, it is invitation only and Dr. Cotta has an invitation plus one and he wants me to go with him!"

"You seem very excited about the invitation to the shop."

"Well, I need to know if it is going to be a rival for ours."

"And Dr. Cotta? Aren't you excited about going with him?"

Mrs. Driscoll turned her head to listen to my reply. "Of course!" I replied with more enthusiasm than I felt. "Dr. Cotta is such good company. I'm sure we'll have a lot of fun and afterwards we're going to *The Imaginarium* for dinner."

"Ooh!" Mrs. Driscoll interrupted. "Let us know what it's like. I've been dying to go since it opened. I've heard such good things about it, especially their puddings."

As Mrs. Driscoll continued to chatter, her conversation turned to shopping and her struggles to find garlic. I listened with a sinking sensation as she related how the village shop had run out of garlic and even a journey to the local town to purchase some for her Bolognese sauce had been futile. "I couldn't find a single bulb, clove, or jar in the shops," she said. "They were even out of puree."

It could only mean one thing; Vlad hadn't kept his promise!

Chapter Eleven

D r. Cotta picked me up from Haligern Cottage at eight-thirty pm. In the days that I hadn't seen him his tan hadn't faded, his dazzling smile hadn't dimmed, and the bright blue of his eyes was still as pure as a cloud-free summer sky. The silver paintwork of the Porsche twinkled in the sunshine and a collective 'ooh' filled the hall as he stepped out of the car and waved to me as I stood on the cottage steps. I felt wholly inadequate in comparison to him and the disparity between his god-like physique and my own dumpy - although my aunts insisted it was curvaceous rather than fat - menopausal figure, hit me like a slap. As I wondered for the hundredth time why a Chris Hemsworth lookalike wanted to bother with a woman like me, I forced a smile and returned his wave. "Right," I said taking a breath and turned to my aunts. "I'll report back later." Despite their prejudice, four pairs of entranced eyes stared beyond me.

"Bye, dear!" Aunt Beatrice said, obviously distracted by the man in the driveway.

"Be careful of the words that you choose, Livitha," Aunt Loveday warned as she caught my gaze. "Your dissembling could easily be thrown into turmoil by a man like that."

Aunt Thomasin tittered. "I imagine she'd rather like that, Loveday!"

"Thomasin!" Aunt Loveday reprimanded. "You know what I mean!"

"Of course, but still ... he is very handsome!" Aunt Thomasin continued, standing on tiptoes to peer over Aunt Loveday's shoulder.

"He's a Cotta!" I heard Aunt Loveday whisper as I stepped down into the driveway.

I glanced back at the women. The attitude towards Dr. Cotta was strikingly similar to that of Garrett Blackwood. According to them, the Blackwood clan were cursed, persona non grata. Was the same then true of Dr. Cotta and his family?

Unaware of their prejudice, he strode across the gravel to meet me, offered his arm as I met him at the bottom of the steps, then walked me to the car.

Despite my anxiety, Dr. Cotta was easy to talk to and by the time we reached the village I felt at ease. Unusually for a late summer evening, the main road was lined with cars and several groups of villagers walked along the paths. A couple passed us as we left the car, called 'Good evening' to Dr. Cotta and continued towards the new shop.

Dusk had fallen and light spilled from the shop's open doorway. From inside came excited chatter and laughter. Two couples stood beside the doorway, each with a champagne flute in hand. The new owner had done a good job of creating a buzz for her evening; the shop was full.

Glasses clinked as we made our way inside. Almost immediately, a waiter appeared and pushed a filled champagne flute into my hand. "Welcome to *Arcane Treasures*. Martha is happy to receive you as her guest this evening." He made a slight bow, then disappeared back into the crowd. A different waiter offered a champagne flute to Dr. Cotta. When he declined, a flute filled with orange juice was offered instead.

The energy within the shop was excited and the guests brimmed with anticipation. I searched the room for the owner but could see no one I didn't recognise from the village. A flashlight popped at the far end of the room and I recognised Keith Cleghorn, the reporter from the Liarton Caller who had harassed us after the sinkhole incident at the village fete. He was taking a photograph of Lady Annabelle Heskitt, a member of the local landed gentry and owner of the nearby stately home. The Reverend Parsivall was chatting to several of the more influential local parishioners along with two members of the Parish Council, a Councillor from the neighbouring town, as well as their mayor. A sense of inferiority wafted over me; I hadn't thought to promote an invitation only evening, or invite the local newspaper, or the local influencers. We were opening in the evening, sure, but we were open to all and I had bought a couple of bottles of white wine, a jar of coffee, a box of tea, and had made three cakes. They were good cakes but weren't on a par with the flutes of champagne or the Michelin grade hors d'oeuvres laid out on silver platters at the side of the room.

The opening of *Haligern Cottage Apothecary* couldn't hope to compete with the elegance and sophistication of this intriguing night.

"Ah! Here she is." The crowd stepped back as though Moses were parting the waves.

Striding towards us, high heels tacking across the trendily stripped and waxed floor, was the most striking woman I had ever seen. Raven black hair cut long but with a fringe just below her brows framed a face with skin as smooth and perfect as alabaster. Large violet eyes lined by thick black lashes sat above high cheekbones coloured with a light dusting of rouge. Full lips were painted a rich red. In a maxi dress of dark plum velvet, her small waist accentuated by a thin belt of dark green silk, she was statuesque and slender, definitely not menopausal, and made a beeline for Dr. Cotta. With a broad smile that showed perfect and immaculately white teeth, she slipped her arm through his, whispered in his ear, then attempted to walk him to the other side of the shop with complete disregard to me. It was obvious that she had not considered I was his 'plus one' for a single second.

"Martha," Dr. Cotta said resisting her pull. "This is Liv. Liv," he smiled down at me, "this is Martha. She owns the shop."

Martha looked down at me as though inspecting an insect and, after a short, judgement-filled moment, said, "Good even-ink, Liv." She held up one perfectly manicured and lily-white hand as though expecting me to take it and kiss it. I took the proffered hand. It was cool to the touch, the flesh a little harder than I had expected. "I am happy to meet you. Please, you must look around my shop. I will borrow Dr. Cotta—just for a moment." Again, she tugged at his arm. Although her English was perfect, her voice held an accent that I thought could perhaps be Russian.

"Liv?" The question was a request for permission, a 'you don't mind, do you?'

"No, it's fine ... I'll be fine."

"You sure?"

"Yes, sure." I managed an affable laugh. "Don't mind me. There's lots to look at."

With her arm now securely hooked through his, Martha walked him to the other side of the room. Standing together, as she whispered, and he smiled, they looked like the perfect power couple—both tall and perfectly proportioned, both beautiful with gleaming smiles. There was no sign of a spreading waistline, sagging boobs, droopy bottom, greying and/or offensively sprouting hair, wrinkling skin, or chaotic hormones, on either of them.

However, despite being abandoned, I was relieved. Whilst both Martha and Dr. Cotta were deep in conversation, I was able to snoop around. Muriel Acaster's fusty shop selling vintage knick-knacks and antiques to the tourists had been transformed.

Soft light fell on the shelves and displays. Glass cabinets and two small chandeliers reflected the light. The walls had been painted chalky white, the flooring stripped back to the original oak floorboards and varnished. Perfectly streak-free glass cabinets sat beside reclaimed pine display units. The walls were hung with original oil paintings in elaborately carved frames painted black. Several depicted medieval war scenes whilst others were portraits of what I thought could be Russian nobility. A huge floor to ceiling mirror in ornate silver frame stood between two massive dressers. Each shelf was lined with black velvet and underlit with soft lights that only added to the intrigue of each arcane and unusual piece. Whilst one dresser was filled with antique jewellery and curios, the other was reserved for items that could be considered magical. A central table held a pyramid of artisan soaps and another dresser held jars and bottles of lotions and salves. Nothing, bar the central table with its soaps and lotions, had a price tag. Whilst the magical items were fascinating, it was the products that could rival our own that had my interest. I inspected lotion in a glass bottle with a pretty label and sighed with relief; on the label was printed 'Bottled in UK. Produce of more than one country'. They were not handmade, not her own recipe, not a real threat to our own concoctions with their herbs gathered under moonlight whilst reciting ancient charms.

As I unscrewed the bottle of lotion to take a sniff of its contents, a familiar face caught my eye and a scurrying figure disappeared through a door at the back of the shop. "Igor!" I whispered as the overly powerful scent hit my nostrils. I twitched my nose and replaced the cap; the lotion was not only intense but carried a synthetic whiff too.

With the bottle back in place, Dr. Cotta and Martha now in conversation with Lady Heskitt, I followed Igor.

Chapter Twelve

After the claustrophobic atmosphere inside the heaving shop, I was relieved to step out into the dark night. Summer was nearing its end and the nights were already beginning to cool. In a few weeks there would be frost on the ground, and the mornings would become dark, the days short, and the Autumn equinox would be with us. Autumn was one of my favourite times of year and this year would be my first as an initiated witch.

Streetlights lit the street beyond the yard but where I stood, the shadows were long. After a quick scan of the area, to ensure that I wasn't seen, I allowed the tingle in my fingers to grow. Light began to glow around my hand until a ball of soft light hovered on my palm. Still amazed by the incredible sight of a ball of light hovering on my palm I shone the light along the walls illuminating the shadows, but Igor wasn't there.

At the far end of the yard a door led out into the street. After a quick glance behind me, I ran to the gate and checked up and down the street. Again, there was no sign of Igor. Conscious that by now Dr. Cotta may have noticed my absence and begun to look for me, I headed back to the shop.

Feet tapped against metal and I noticed movement above me. Igor was making his way down a flight of metal steps from an apartment above the shop. Intrigued, I stood back in the shadows, reducing the light in my palm to a tiny flicker, and watched him descend. He grunted with effort, weighed down by a large sack slung over his hunched and elderly shoulders. As he stepped onto the ground, he took a moment to catch his breath, readjusted the heavy bag and began to head for the gate at the rear of the property. As far as I knew, Igor wasn't familiar with anyone in the village. It meant only one thing. Igor was a thief and he had to be stopped!

"Igor!" I hissed.

Jumping out of the shadows, I bounded across the yard with my witch-light brightening. Startled, and blinded by the now intense light, he threw an arm across his face. He grunted something in Romanian – which I had discovered was his native language and where the Count originated from, or at least where Wikipedia said that Transylvania was. His words were unintelligible to me, but expletives have the same tone in any language!

"Igor!" I said, breathless as I skidded to a stop. "Put it back!"

He continued to grumble then slapped at my hand.

"Sorry!" I dimmed the light emanating from my palm to a low glow that still illuminated his face. "It turned up by itself," I said, explaining the sudden brightness. "I'm not used to it yet."

My apology was followed by more mumbled expletives and he turned to the gate. "You did not see me here," he said with a dramatic arc of his hand.

For a moment I thought he was attempting to cast some sort of memory or invisibility spell. "Nope," I said, "I can still see you."

He grunted. "No! You did not see me here," he insisted.

"Still not working!"

"Femeie proastă!"

"Can you repeat that in English, please? I'm sorry, I'm not good at languages."

"Certainly, Miss Erikson. I said, 'stupid woman'!"

"Oh." My cheeks began to burn. "Sorry!"

"Always with the 'sorry'!" he sighed. "You should not always say the 'sorry'. I insulted you!" He jabbed a bony finger at me. "You should be angry. A woman should slap the face of a man who is rude!"

"Oh ..." I bit back the 'sorry' that wanted to spill from my lips, unsure whether he was inviting me to actually slap him, decided he wasn't, then said, "Okay ... anyway ..." I made an effort to sound authoritative and pointed at the bag. "You've got to put that back."

"You've got to put that back," Igor mimicked with a wheedling voice.

Did I really sound that pathetic? Was the fat little mouse still in residence?

"No! You must say it with force—like you mean it. I have lived with the Count for many years, decades, and I have learned a few things ..."

"I bet you have," I said. "But you can't steal people's stuff."

"I, Igor Nicolae Țăranu, do not steal!" He spat on the floor for emphasis.

"But you've just been into that apartment, which I know does not belong to you, and now have a bag on your back. You look exactly like a burglar escaping with a bag of loot!" It occurred to me then that Igor was completely out of place at the open evening. "Igor, what are you even doing here? It's an invitation only event and I saw you inside?"

"You don't think Igor is good enough to be invited?"

"No! I-"

"No?"

"Sorry! I didn't mean it like that. I meant, no, I do think you're good enough.

"That makes no sense!"

"Okay, sorry! Then, yes, of course you're good enough."

He seemed mollified.

"So, how come you are invited?" I persisted. "I wasn't invited—not personally at least."

"I'm working," he said bluntly.

"Theft is not work!"

"You insult me again. You think because I am the servant of the Count that I must be a lowly thief!"

"No! No, of course not." I got the impression that I was being played. "But tell me then, what are you doing if not stealing?"

"I told you—working."

"Has the Count put you up to this? Is he here?" I asked looking round for tell-tale signs of Vlad.

"Psht!" Igor hissed. "No!" his voice was a hoarse whisper. "He does not know I am here."

"Oh? Then how can you be working?"

"You never saw me here!" he said with another dramatic sweep of his hand.

It was obvious that Igor didn't want to divulge the real reason for being in the apartment, so I decided to play it tough.

"Tell me, Igor Nicolae Ţăranu, why you are here, or I will have to call the police."

"Pah!"

He was unimpressed by my threat. I tried a different authority. "Then, I shall tell the Count."

"No!" There was genuine fear in his voice. Guilt rose but I pushed it down. "Well, tell me the truth."

"I am working for Martha."

"Martha! The woman who owns the shop?"

"Yes."

"But why?"

"I am bored!" He said this with relief. "For decades I have served the Count. Night after night it is the same—light the candles, bring his slippers. Decade after decade I have listened to him talking about Mina and walking in the shadows!" He huffed with irritated resignation. "Martha needed my help setting up the shop so ..."

"So, that's where you've been sloping off to."

"Yes."

"Well ..." I wasn't sure what to say but decided it was none of my business. Certainly, if he had been with the Count for decades, I could understand his grievances. Plus, Igor wasn't doing anything illegal, and he was a grown man capable of making his own decisions. It was up to him how he ran his life. "Okay, Igor. I never saw you here."

For the first time since his arrival, a genuine smile, rather than a loaded smirk, rose on his face and I saw a flicker of the younger man he once was. He grunted and turned back to the gate. It was only as he stepped through the gateway, and the streetlight illuminated his back, that I noticed movement from within the bag!

Loud chatter and low music filtered into the yard, and the back door opened as I struggled to process the image of a squirming bag slung over Igor's shoulder.

"Liv!"

Surprised to hear my voice called, I quickly extinguished the witch light still hovering around my hand and replied, "Hi! Yes, it's me."

Dr. Cotta stepped into the yard just as Igor disappeared into the shadows. "What're you doing out here? I've been looking for you."

"I just needed some fresh air." It wasn't a complete lie.

"Yeah, it is a bit stuffy in there." He took my arm and guided me back inside. "Come on. I've told Martha all about your shop and she's dying to meet you."

Chapter Thirteen

The crowd had not thinned as I returned to the busy room and another glass of champagne was thrust at me as we made our way through. I took a sip then held my glass aloft as Dr. Cotta manoeuvred us through the throngs of people until we stood in front of Martha. Violet eyes caught me in their trap as the impossibly elegant woman focused down on me.

Her first words were like a slap. "You are *very* popular, Livitha, with the local men."

"Pardon!" I was taken aback, unsure if I'd heard her correctly.

She repeated her statement, her violet eyes holding mine without blinking.

I scrabbled for a suitable response. "Well, I wouldn't say that. Dr. Cotta's new and I'm just helping him settle in." I was floundering, but Dr. Cotta offered me a reassuring smile and showed no sign of slight.

"I bet that you are!" She raised a knowing brow. "And what about him?" She gestured to a tall man with dark hair looking our way.

"Garrett!" I blurted his name before I had a chance to stop myself.

"He seems very interested in you too." She followed this with a small laugh.

Garrett looked away, pretending to inspect one of the arcane artifacts from the velvet covered shelf holding occult items. He held up a box and offered it to the large blonde at his side. She took it, inspecting it with interest. Bewilderment slapped me. Garrett had been staring in my direction, but he was with another woman. My fingers began to fizz, the pain was intense, but I forced a smile. Martha eyed me keenly as though I were a particularly interesting specimen about to perform some novel behaviour.

"Garrett's just an old friend," I said, acutely aware of Dr. Cotta by my side. He too was now watching my reaction. "We were at school together. He's probably just thinking how old I've got since he last saw me." I stroked the white streak of hair.

"Hmm!" Martha's lips pressed together as though repressing a laugh. "I think it suits you. Very much like the 'Bride of Frankenstein.'"

Dr. Cotta laughed. "It is a striking look, Liv, and Martha's right, it does suit you."

"Thanks." I was now completely on edge. Being the centre of attention was something I hated. I was the kind of child who would hide behind the other kids whenever we put on a play at school, desperate to melt into the background. Other kids would fight over who would play the lead parts whilst I would pray to be the tree. I fingered the lock of white hair, forced a smile in a desperate effort to appear chilled enough to accept a compliment then searched my mind for something interesting to say. The embers at my core were beginning to spark into life and I was conscious of waves of heat rising through my body. Typical! This was the absolute worst time to have a menopausal hot flush, but here it was, my body letting me down, ambushing me again. I was on the cusp of panic and desperate to excuse myself when Dr. Cotta slipped an arm across my shoulders and gave me a slight squeeze. It should have been a comfort but given the newness of our friendship and my uneasy emotional state, I flinched. He made no indication of noticing my reaction and instead said, "Liv's the one who's going to be managing the apothecary shop just down the road."

"Ah! Is that the little shop that has just been newly renovated? It is so quaint!"

Despite her smiles, referring to the apothecary as quaint seemed to demean it, and I sensed that the shop, like me, was not quite up to par with Martha's standards. I became Marjorie Babcock's 'little fat mouse' in an instant. "Thanks." I managed a smile. "It is smaller than your shop, but we like it."

Her eyes glittered as she took me in, and I got the distinct impression that she was picking up on my unease, perhaps even understanding and fanning my rising sense of inadequacy. I also got the distinct impression that she was holding her tongue in front of Dr. Cotta; she wanted to impress him, not appear as a snidey competitor. The woman's energy was toxic!

"And you are opening tomorrow?"

Garrett moved to the other side of the shop. His 'plus one' followed.

Distracted by Garrett, Martha's question filtered slowly through to my awareness. Martha focused on my face as she waited for my reply. "Sorry! Yes! We have an open evening tomorrow."

"Ah! You are having one too!"

There it was! An accusation of imitation.

"We've been planning it for weeks!" I sounded defensive. Dr. Cotta coughed, obviously picking up on the uneasiness of our conversation. A triumphant glitter flashed in her eyes and disbelief curled onto her lips. I hated her in an instant. "It's not going to be as glamorous as yours, I'm afraid," I heard myself say. "But we will have cake."

"Bonza, Liv!" Dr. Cotta said with encouragement. "What kind of cake?"

Garrett caught my eye then quickly looked away and, put on the spot in front of this uber-chic woman, I struggled to remember. "Well ..." *Chocolate!* "We have chocolate, and vanilla ..." My cheeks began to burn! I sounded pathetic, as did my cakes, and my lacklustre response was casting a damp blanket over our grand opening.

"Sounds ... delicious!" Martha said with an indulgent smile. "You must have worked ... awfully hard."

I liked her even less, but I hated myself more in that moment. I was lame, an also-ran who could never hope to rise to her level of sophistication.

Martha gave a small nod that signalled the end of our conversation, then moved away but not before taking hold of Dr. Cotta's arm and whispering to him. I was dismissed. A non-entity. A disappointment. Heat seared my cheeks. I was an idiot, fumbling for words, put on tenterhooks by my own lack of confidence—again! As I watched her walk away, my faculties returned. "Actually," I called to her back as she slid with ease and grace through the crowd, "we've made an espresso, chocolate & chilli cake with coffee cream, a chocolate & Earl Grey torte, and a raspberry chocolate cake with Chambord ganache!"

She turned momentarily, offered me a wave and superior smile, then continued towards a group of wealthy-looking men. Garrett followed her momentarily with his eyes, then ours met. He gave a small wave and a slight smile.

"They sound delicious, Liv," Dr. Cotta said and slipped his arm through mine. Garrett's smile dropped. My belly churned. A bead of sweat trickled at my temple and I fought to hold back the panic-induced heat that signalled a huge power surge charging at my core. I had to get out of the shop. The last time I had felt this close to spontaneous combustion my magick had hit the ancient oak at Haligern making it blossom with peonies. Incredibly beautiful as that sight had been, it had been a private affair. An explosion of magick here would be disastrous. It would damage the shop and I would be outed as a witch or, at the very least, a freak!

"Can we go outside?" I begged. "I'm desperate for some fresh air."

"Sure, we need to leave anyway. I booked dinner at *The Imaginarium* and we're already late!"

The evening hadn't got off to a great start, but there was worse to come!

Chapter Fourteen

Ordering spaghetti was a mistake.

No matter how many times I tried to wrap the long strings of pasta around my fork, they would spring apart and dangle below my chin each time I opened my mouth. More than once I'd had to dab my chin with the serviette and it was becoming blotched with the Bolognese sauce. Dr. Cotta had made the sensible choice of steak and sat in perfect composure, looking intensely handsome and self-assured as I struggled through my bowl of pasta. I sprinkled on another handful of parmesan in the hope that it would help bind the wayward spaghetti but after another failed attempt that Dr. Cotta ignored in gentlemanly fashion, I gave up and cut the pasta up into short child-friendly lengths! It was another failure to add to tonight's growing list.

With wine glasses re-filled, he raised his glass. I raised my own.

"To you, Livitha Erikson," he said with a smile, "who is making my move to England so much more interesting!"

"Oh! Well, I'm glad to be able to help. I imagine Martha is helping too!" Alcohol was loosening my tongue, and I was unable to hold back a dig about Martha and her obvious attraction to him. "She seemed to like you."

"Oh, Martha? Yeah, she's attractive, but I get the impression she'd be hard work! Anyway, she's in some sort of complicated relationship, but I think she's searching for Mr. Right. She said something about searching for the man she loved. Dunno! Anyway," he took another sip of wine and encouraged me to do the same. "I'd much rather talk about you!"

After two glasses of champagne at Martha's shop, I was beginning to feel a little heady.

"So, Liv, tell me about your aunts."

"Oh." I had not expected that question.

"I've told you a fair bit about my family, and now I'd love to learn about yours."

"Well ... what do you want to know?"

"You've told me so little ..."

"Well, I'm separated, you know that ... and ... I live with my aunts."

"Quite the little coven!"

I was taken aback by his remark and hoped that my surprise didn't show. I took another sip of wine whilst looking beyond his shoulder, avoiding eye contact. "I'm not sure my aunts would be happy you thought that."

"Oh, you know I'm only joking. It's just unusual to find such a large group of women living together."

"I guess, but it's what's normal for me. When my parents died, my aunts rallied and took care of me. I guess they decided being together was the easiest thing to do."

"And they're all unmarried? Apart from Aunt Loveday?"

"Yes, that's right." My head began to buzz, and I was conscious that I could easily slip into telling him too much. "Raif has been like a father to me."

Foolishly, I took another sip of wine, then drained the glass. Dr. Cotta refilled it. I began to feel so much more at ease and took another sip. Tonight had been difficult and my anxiety had shot through the roof, but the wine, and Dr. Cotta's easy smile, were certainly helping.

The conversation continued with Dr. Cotta asking more questions about Haligern and my aunts, about my childhood, and my marriage to Pascal. At no point was he judgemental or mocking and we sank into easy conversation. I even managed to tell a joke that by some miracle he found amusing. Towards the bottom of my second large glass of wine, the bell above the door tinkled but it was the change on Dr. Cotta's face that finally got my attention. With his eyes focused on an approaching figure, he began to rise. I turned. Vlad was striding across the room, his focus entirely on Dr. Cotta. The room swayed and I felt a little dizzy. Vlad looked slightly fuzzy as he reached the table, if not peculiar in a lumberjack style plaid jacket and burgundy peaked cap.

"Good even-ink Livitha. Introduce me to your dinner companion."

"Good even-ink, Vlad." I smiled.

His lips pursed. "You have been drinking, I see," he said with disapproval.

"Just a little. Only two glasses of wine."

He sniffed. "So, who is it that is plying you with alcohol?" He fixed his eyes on Dr. Cotta.

"You're not my dad, Vlad!" I giggled then pressed my lips together. I had had too much to drink.

Vlad turned his attention to Dr. Cotta. "I am a family friend. I am here to make sure Livitha is being taken care of."

"Well ... I can assure you that she is."

"You care for this wonderful woman by getting her drunk!"

He called me wonderful!

"Well ... she's a grown woman, she can drink what she likes," Dr. Cotta returned. Although he was growing defensive, his voice was still placatory.

"A woman who is going through a divorce is vulnerable. I should not like to see a many preying on that vulnerability."

Someone at another table tittered.

"Shh!" I whispered. "They're listening." I poured myself a glass of water and drank a large mouthful. "See, I'm not drunk." Mortification was sobering me fast.

"Please ... Vlad, won't you join us?" Dr. Cotta indicated a chair. I threw Vlad a pleading glance. He sat in the chair, though remained stiffly upright, and continued to assess Dr. Cotta.

"Forgive me, I am old-fashioned."

For a moment I thought he was going to launch into his spiel about walking through the shadows, but instead he said, "Livitha is dear to me. I should not like her to come to harm."

"I can assure you that whilst she is with me, it won't."

The Count nodded and I caught a flicker of red in his eye as he said, "I trust that it will not, or you will have me to answer to. Now," he said with a look of grim determination, "she is to be home by eleven o'clock. Is that understood?"

For a moment I thought that Dr. Cotta was going to become angry and refuse Vlad's orders, but instead he simply nodded. "Understood."

"Good, then I leave."

With a tip of his baseball cap, Vlad left the restaurant. I waited for some sort of backlash from Dr. Cotta, but apart from a slightly drawn brow, he only said, "Well, Martha was right. You are popular with the men in this village." He raised his glass, chinked it against mine, and then we both burst out laughing.

"I am so sorry! I have no idea what has come over him. He's not usually so protective."

"It was ... quaint, although I have to admit he is rather terrifying! His eyes looked so ... so ..."

"Piercing?" I offered.

"I was going to say soulless, but piercing is about right too!" He laughed again although the laughter faded from his eyes as he looked through the window to the street.

I took another sip of water then ordered a coffee determined to sober up. Our meal continued and when the pudding menu was brought across, I ordered the homemade jam roly-poly with custard - which Mrs Driscoll had heard was delicious - whilst Dr. Cotta had a huge slice of banoffee pie with ice cream. By the end of the meal, I felt far more sober. We ordered coffee then sat back to relax and enjoy the rest of the time we had left. The bell tinkled again, and this time Dr. Cotta waved to the newcomer.

To my surprise, Reverend Parsivall not only walked over to our table, but pulled out a chair and sat down, then placed a file on the table.

"Sorry to interrupt your evening, John, and ... Liv, isn't it?" I nodded.

"I hope you'll forgive me for bringing the office to you, but I have some papers that need signing." He tapped the folder.

What could possibly need signing at this time of night?

Dr. Cotta didn't refuse, question, or even seem surprised, but instead took the pen Parsivall offered then proceeded to sign the paperwork after only a cursory glance.

Job done, Parsivall stood, tipped me a nod, thanked me for my patience then disappeared.

Odd! This evening was turning out to be peculiar. "So, I don't like to ask, but I will, because I'm nosey," I said trying to make a joke of my intense desire to know exactly what paperwork had just been signed, "but what was that about?"

Dr. Cotta narrowed his eyes, took a breath, then said, "Okay, Liv, I'll tell you, but to be honest, it's not something I'd tell everyone because I guess I could get in trouble—signing that kind of stuff out of hours. It's confidential you see, but we're friends, and I know I can trust you."

Wow! My interest was piqued. "Go on," I said in a half-interested way that I hoped seemed casual.

"It was a death certificate."

I was not expecting that. "But aren't you supposed to check that someone's dead first."

"Oh, I know they're dead, it's just the paperwork got snarled up. Parsival was just helping out."

I have to admit, I knew nothing about the formalities of death.

"He's an amazing, guy. He does a lot of work for the local hospice and hospitals and offers his services as a death doula."

"What is a death doula?"

"They sit with the dying as they pass."

"Oh!"

"Yeah, Parsivall jokes that he's their 'friend at the end'! He spends a lot of his spare time at hospices. He's in real demand. There are a lot of lonely people out there, Liv."

I shuddered. "It's kind of creepy."

Dr. Cotta laughed. "Well, I guess you could see it like that, but Reverend Parsivall gives people a lot of ... courage, I guess ... when they need it most. He's a kind guy, Liv. One of the good ones."

I nodded, though my feelings were at odds with Dr. Cotta's words. But, if what Dr. Cotta said was right, then I had misjudged the Reverend Parsivall. After being fooled by Pascal for so long, I was beginning to realise that getting people wrong was a skill I excelled in.

"He sees the thing all the way through to the very end then afterwards he takes care of the funerals. You'd be surprised at how many people don't have family or can't afford a proper funeral. He makes it real nice for them, but then he owns the funeral home, so he can swallow some of the costs. Sometimes he doesn't make any profit at all. That's what I call a good guy!"

That's what I'd call a conflict of interests! "One of the best by the sound of it!" I smiled and took another sip of coffee.

Chapter Fifteen

B ack at home, I pondered the evening or, rather, ruminated on my failures and went to bed claiming a headache. Worried glances were exchanged between my aunts when I promised to give them details about Martha's shop and her open evening in the morning. I was in a sudden slump. The past weeks had been a roller-coaster ride, from discovering I was a witch with nascent and, at times, overwhelming powers, to leaving my husband and being accused of murder, then being chased through the forest by men on a witch hunt intent on burning me at the stake, followed by being attacked by a grotesque imp from the dark realms. On top of that I had been busy organising the opening of my aunts' apothecary shop. It was a big deal to them. They would finally have a public face in the village after decades – centuries actually – of being hidden away. Now, it looked as though the special night I had planned, imagined for the past weeks, and fretted over endlessly, would be a damp squib. I couldn't hope to rival Martha's glittering evening and the comparison between hers and ours would be fresh in people's minds.

My head thumped.

I had to do something to make it special!

I also had to do something to get me out of this funk of misery before it settled into something worse. My menopausal hormones were just another 'issue' I had to deal with. Night sweats, a profusion of wiry hairs in all the wrong places, hot flashes just at the wrong time, weight that just wouldn't shift and clung to my middle as though it were a life belt growing in readiness should I ever fall into the water, were bad enough, but perhaps worst of all were the mood swings. I could go from laid back and hopeful to climbing the walls with irritation and overdosing on anxiety. It was as though someone had flipped a switch, or given me an injection of stress hormones, but at least I recognised it.

I regretted now not sharing my feelings with my aunts – Aunt Euphemia was bound to have some pacifying elixir to help. I decided on a bit of self-care to try and buoy my mood. First, I made an effort to focus my attention on something other than this evening's failures, but the scent of Martha's shop seemed impregnated in my clothes and the odour of spaghetti Bolognese wafted from my hair. Worse though was the lingering scent of Dr. Cotta's aftershave on my cheek where he'd leaned in to bid me goodnight with a kiss. I cringed as the memory of his lips touching my cheek was juxtaposed with Garrett's sombre face as he noticed my 'plus one'. I rubbed at my cheek and almost ran to the bathroom.

After showering, and scrubbing every inch of my body, I wafted my hair dry then ensured any lingering scent was blocked by giving my wrists and chest a liberal spray of my favourite perfume, Chanel No. 5. Scrubbed clean and doused in expensive perfume, I settled back on my pillows and scrolled through my Kindle's virtual library for something to read.

Scratching from the other side of my door announced Lucifer's arrival. Like any cat, he enjoyed his comforts and one of his favourite places to curl up and sleep was the end of my bed, or middle if he was being annoying, or the pillow if he was being particularly obnoxious.

"Come on in, then," I said as I opened the door.

"About time!" he said with an imperious tip of his head. "I've been waiting."

"Yes, for all of about ten seconds," I replied. He was in one of those moods!

He trotted across to my bed jumped into the middle and stretched himself out exactly where my legs would be. "Shift over," I said as I pulled the cover back with a gentle tug. He mewled and rolled over as though I had yanked the duvet. I sighed and waited for the inevitable confrontation.

"Be careful!" he yowled.

"Lucifer!" I sighed. I was in no mood for his belligerence but couldn't let him get away with accusing me of being rough towards him.

"I could have been thrown off the bed. You could have given me a concussion."

"Lucifer! That's simply not true," I said as I got back into bed, pushing my legs beneath the cat.

"Now she's kicking me!"

"Lucifer! I did not."

"Did!"

"Listen, I've had a difficult evening, I'm tired, and the last thing I need is you coming in here and picking a fight."

"How very dare you! I would not *pick* a fight." He sniffed the air. "What is that smell?"

"Chanel No. 5!" I said, smelling my wrist then holding it out for him. "Take a sniff."

He sniffed, twitched his nose, then said. "No, that's not it. There's something else. Something ... smelly!"

"Very descriptive."

He jumped off the bed. I scanned the room, worried now that the fairies had returned or perhaps some other wild animal had found a way in. Living in the countryside, surrounded by woodlands and fields, it wasn't unheard of for mice to take up residence. One year, a mouse had made a nest under the kitchen sink and the first we'd known about it was when a troupe of scurrying and tiny baby mice ran across the tiles.

"It's not fairies, is it?"

He ignored me and sauntered across to the clothes I had worn that evening and now draped across a chair. He sniffed at my shirt. "Pooh!"

"What is it?"

"It stinks. Particularly around the armpits."

A flush crept to my cheeks. "Thanks!"

"It's sour. Did you not enjoy this evening, Livitha? Your clothes reek!"

"I spilt a little spaghetti Bolognese that's all."

"No, it's not food. I have superior olfactory senses; I can smell a mouse, or a fairy, at fifty paces, if not more, and your clothes stink of something far worse than pasta sauce. In fact, the sauce smells rather nice. No, there's a reek about your clothes that stinks of fear, so, I ask again, how did your evening go?"

I listened with a slack jaw. "If you must know, it was difficult."

"You were afraid? Was there something chasing you? Did you fear for your life?"

"No, not exactly, but there was this woman and then Garrett turned up."

"Ah, Blackwood."

"And ..." I wanted to tell him about Igor and the sack on his back but wasn't sure I could trust him not to open his mouth at the wrong time. "And the shop ... her open evening, was just so ... impressive, I guess, and ours won't be anywhere near as good!"

"How dare you!"

I had expected sympathy. "Pardon?"

"How dare you underestimate the love that this village has for your aunts! No newcomer, no matter how beautiful or glamorous or glitzy could ever trump the centuries of work that they have poured into this community. You insult them, Livitha!"

"I-"

"No! I won't hear another word. Your opening tomorrow will be a success, however low key it is. You may not have champagne or bright sparkling lights, and you may not be as ... svelte as she, or as charismatic, or fascinating, or beautiful-"

"Alright! I get it!"

"Or rich, but you have other qualities ..." I waited for him to elaborate, but he didn't. "And you have your aunts; no one could better those delightful women!"

"Sure, but-"

He held up a paw and fixed me with glowering green eyes. "I will not hear another negative comment."

I pressed my lips together, his words churning over, scalding me with their ire, then I fixed him with a glare of my own.

"Lucifer, how do you know that the new owner is beautiful and charismatic?"

"Oh, just a guess," he replied. "You were so ... down and full of self-pity, it was obvious that you felt inferior and I know you Liv, plus you're easy to read, textbook really. You have so little self-esteem that coming across another woman and, in this case, it has to be admitted, a far more attractive and slender one than yourself, gives you a knock."

"Right."

"Now, don't start moping again, you've been the solitary guest of your own pity-party far too many times over the years!"

"I see, well thanks for the pep talk!"

"Don't mention it," Lucifer replied, oblivious, or more likely indifferent, to my sarcasm. He jumped back onto my bed, pawed the fabric, then curled up on my knees. "Now, be a dear and turn off the light. I've had a busy day."

Chapter Sixteen

I woke several hours later with the Kindle on my chest, my glasses pressing into my nose, Lucifer a weight on my shins, and scratching coming from the window followed by irritated rapping on the glass.

Pulling the curtains revealed a floating, and obviously annoyed, vampire. Vlad hovered outside my window, rapping again on the glass as I gestured for him to go to his own room.

Once again, the window to Vlad's room was locked and I was the object of his accusation.

"Why did you do it, Livitha?"

"Do what? I haven't done anything!"

"Lock me out. This is the second time! The first time I forgive, but this! This is unforgiveable."

His eyes glowered.

"I didn't lock you out! I swear. I've been out all evening. You know that."

"Pah! I think it is revenge!"

"Of course it's not."

"I am only trying to protect you. You are a vulnerable woman. You have a terrible history with men!"

"What? I've only been married once."

"And you let him make a fool of you for years. He had countless women. Took mistresses right under your nose and

101

you didn't suspect a thing. He was vainglorious, a cheating phi-landerer!"

"You've been talking to my aunts."

"Well ... yes. And, as they told me of your sorrows, I knew I had to become your protector!"

They had obviously painted a pathetic picture of me. "Vlad, I appreciate your ... help, but honestly, I'm okay. Dr. Cotta is just a friend."

"Hah! Men do not take women out to dinner for friend-ship!"

"Well ..." He continued to stare at me, his eyes glittering, and then I noticed the mark on his collar. At first I thought it was blood and I took a step back. "Vlad, I thought you said you would behave yourself whilst you were here."

"And I have."

"Have? As in the past tense?"

"Am, then! I *am* behaving myself. I have not bitten anyone in the village."

"What about the next town?"

"Nor the next town."

"Then what is that on your collar? It looks like blood."

"Impossible!"

I took a step closer. Red was smeared across the fabric and there was a patch on his neck too. The patch glistened with a pinkish tinge. Blood would have congealed and perhaps even begun to dry and turn brown. "Is that ... lipstick?"

He looked surprised before checking the wall beyond my shoulder with sudden interest.

It was! "Vlad? Is it lipstick? Because you said you weren't going to do that kind of thing—at least not whilst you were here, out of respect for my aunts!"

"What are you accusing me of! I have just told you that I have not bitten anyone! Is my word not good enough? Are you calling me a liar?"

"No! Of course not, but … if people started turning up dead it would cause … trouble!" I said with massive understatement.

"I will not bring trouble to your door. I, Vlad Dracul have given my solemn promise!"

I wasn't one hundred percent sure that a vampire's word was good, but I was sure I wanted to know how the lipstick had ended up on his collar. "So, if you didn't bite a woman … or a man …."

"Women! I only bite women!"

"So, if you didn't bite a woman and that isn't blood but lipstick, then how did it get there?"

"I kissed a woman! There! Are you satisfied?"

I sensed I could push him a little further. "Well … not really. Who is she? Do you know her name?"

"Of course I know her name! I do not kiss strange women! What kind of man do you take me for?"

A remorseless blood-sucking vampire! "I didn't mean to offend, Vlad," I said and took a friendly, interested tone. "So, this is exciting!" It was certainly intriguing. From everything I knew about vampires, much gleaned from films, but some from my experience with Vlad, they were far keener on using their powers of suggestion to entrance a woman. This was new behaviour as far as I was aware. "Tell me all about it!" I said this as though Vlad were one of my single girlfriends about to fill me in on the details of her latest date. "What's her name?"

He looked a little taken aback. "Well ... her name is Mindy ..."

"And where did you meet her?"

"The morgue."

"Oh!" I wasn't sure how to react to that revelation. "So, was she ... visiting?" The image of Vlad stalking a fog-filled cemetery sprang to mind.

"No. She works there. She is a morgue technician."

"Oh. I see. That must be an interesting job!" I struggled to respond.

"It is!" He said with a gleam in his eye. "She has talked to me about it a lot. It is fascinating what is done to the bodies of the dead. Although, she has applied for a job at a different morgue."

I hid a grimace; talking about death, thinking about death and its inevitable destruction of the body, weren't comfortable topics for me. "So ... Mindy ... from the morgue ... you haven't bitten her?"

"No!"

"But isn't that a little ... unusual for you?"

"Yes!" He sighed with relief. "Yes, it is! Oh, it is so good to be able to talk to someone about it." With that, the Count threw his cape onto the sofa, gestured for me to sit, and then explained how he had met 'Mindy from the Morgue' on a moonlit night as he had taken a walk. She was unlike any other woman he had met. There were no screams as he approached, no fainting, no horror-filled eyes, just intrigue. "I have not come across a woman like this since I met my Mina! She understands me in a way no other woman – apart from my Mina – does!"

"If that's the case, then how come you haven't made her one of your 'brides'."

"We're dating."

"Dating?"

"Yes! I want to get to know her."

This was new!

"I am not sure I want her to be one of my brides, Livitha. At least not yet. She is funny. She makes me laugh. All my other wives—they ..." He groaned. "I am a passionate man, Livitha. Always I jump in too soon, and each time I am burned – not literally you understand – but they nag and nag or argue or whine! It is hell at the castle! I want this to be different. Until I find my Mina, I need a companion, someone I can really talk to."

"And Mindy is that companion?"

"I am hoping so!"

I studied the Count, lost for words. He had just leapt up-wards in my estimation. "Well, if she makes you laugh, then I think that bodes well," I managed.

"It does, Livitha. I am so happy that you understand! We are similar creatures, you and I, both wronged by love. It is why I feel compelled to protect you." To my surprise, he placed an arm across my shoulder. "One day, you will be together with your soulmate, as I will be with mine."

He sighed and I sensed that the Count was about to slip into reminiscing. From past conversations I knew I would be trapped for hours unless I made a quick exit. I thanked him for sharing his news with me, suggested he bring Mindy to the opening, then made my excuses and returned to my own bed.

Eyes burning, my mind filled with images from the evening, I fell into a deep sleep and dreamed of Garrett and the woman in the woods. Garret placed a stick on the fire beneath her cauldron and sparks flew, morphing into brilliant stars that filled a raven-black sky. However, as I woke, my dream was filled with Martha. Fabulous in black velvet, a tiara sparkling in the light from a thousand candles, Vlad held her as they danced at the centre of a vast ballroom, and I was infused with the certainty that Martha was in fact a reincarnation of Mina!

Chapter Seventeen

That evening was *Haligern Cottage Apothecary's* grand opening, but my mind was filled with thoughts of Martha and Vlad. The more I thought about the pair, the more certain I was that they were soulmates, fated to search for one another time after time. I had woken not only with dreams but sodden with hormonal sweats, so showered then checked my complexion for signs of any unwanted hair sprouting from my chin or upper lip, used my reading glasses and a magnifying mirror to double check, then made my way downstairs.

A fire had already been lit in the hearth and steam rose from the cauldron hanging from chains above it. Aunt Thomasin recited a charm as she stirred then smiled as she caught my eye. "Come, Livitha, add your magick to my work." This was another first for me, but I joined her at the hearth. She placed my hand on the wooden spoon. "Now, recite-"

A mess of potatoes and carrots bubbled in the pot. "But this is stew!"

"It is." She let out a small cackle.

"So why are we reciting a charm?"

"It's one of Euphemia's stews. It needs all the help it can get!"

Aunt Beatrice snorted at the sink, her shoulders heaving.

Aunt Euphemia made delicious wines, preserves, and jams, her lotions were potent and could clear up the worst acne within days, but she was a notoriously terrible cook.

"That's rotten!" I chided.

"It is," she laughed. "Which is why it needs help."

"No, I meant tricking me was rotten. I'm sure the stew will taste lovely." I doubted that but didn't want to be disloyal to my aunt.

Aunt Thomasin chuckled then threw in a pinch of salt and ground some pepper into the pot. "There, that should help."

Footsteps in the hallway sent Aunt Thomasin scurrying to the pantry where she made a pretence of tidying the shelves. Aunt Euphemia walked across to the cauldron and stirred the bubbling stew.

Aunt Beatrice's shoulders heaved. "I must milk Old Mawde!" She grabbed the tin pail and disappeared through the back door.

I busied myself with the coffee pot trying not to listen to Aunt Thomasin failing to hold in her giggles in the pantry.

"Tsk! Tsk! Thomasin. If you think I don't know what you're up to, then you are sillier than I thought."

"What was that, Euphemia?"

"Pah!" Euphemia batted a hand in the direction of the pantry. "They think I'm just a silly old woman, but I know what they're laughing at. I know." She continued to mumble then added a large handful of seasoning to the stew. I held back a groan; it was bound to taste awful now.

After feeding Lucifer - and this time refusing point blank to give him port before nine am - I poured a cup of coffee and sat at the table. Cutting into a freshly baked bread bun, I spread it liberally with butter and marmalade, then broached the subject that my mind refused to stop thinking about just as Aunt Beatrice returned with a fresh pail of goat's milk.

"So, I've been thinking ..."

"Steady!" Again, Aunt Thomasin chuckled. Her mood this morning was certainly mischievous.

"About Vlad."

Three pairs of eyes widened. I had their complete attention.

"He's a married man, Livitha!"

"A little too old for you!"

I tried to correct them, but my words were lost in the barrage of opinions.

"I think he likes his women a little younger, Liv!"

"What does that matter? He's a vampire. She a witch. It is unthinkable."

"I thought you liked Dr. Cotta?"

"Well Vlad may be an improvement on Cotta?"

"What!" I blurted. How on earth could Vlad be an improvement on the exceedingly good looking Dr. Cotta?

"Hmm. You may be right."

"You can't be serious?" Again, my words went unheeded.

"It's irrelevant! Vlad is a vampire and Liv is a witch!"

At that moment Aunt Loveday entered the kitchen. "What is all this commotion?" she said as my aunts continued their heated exchange. I sat back stunned at the level of emotion I had stirred. It was erroneous of course, but my aunts were so intent on expressing their distaste at the idea of me and Vlad as a couple that it was impossible to get a word in edgeways and correct them.

"Vlad and Livitha!"

Aunt Loveday turned to stare at me. I bit down into my marmalade laden bread, now almost enjoying the commotion.

"Vlad and Livitha?" Astonished, her eyes widened. "But Livitha, you are a witch, and he, he is a vampire!"

My mouth full of bread and marmalade, I shrugged my shoulders in a non-committal way.

"It is forbidden!" Aunt Euphemia said with passion.

"I don't think it is entirely forbidden, Euphemia," Aunt Loveday replied with her gaze still on me. A quizzical, disbelieving frown had fallen across her face.

"Well, I forbid it!" Aunt Euphemia said with passion. "It's ... it's just not right."

I met Aunt Loveday's gaze with wide, innocent, eyes and continued to eat my bread. She narrowed hers. I held back laughter. A tiny smile curved at the corner of her mouth. "Well, I think that having Vlad as a son-in-law wouldn't be that bad ..." Mirth glittered in her eyes. I raised my brows, laughter barely hidden by the bread bun.

"Well! I ... I'm not sure I could tolerate ... Raif would hit the roof, Loveday!" Aunt Euphemia spluttered.

Loveday returned with, "When Cupid's arrow strikes ..."

"You cannot be serious ... Oh, Livitha ..."

"If she really does love him ... perhaps we should ... consider the union?" Aunt Beatrice said with resignation.

At that I burst out laughing. "Oh, you are the worst!"

"What have you been telling them, Livitha?" Aunt Loveday asked.

"All I said was that I had been thinking about Vlad. They didn't let me finish."

"Just presumed you were romantically involved?"

"Yes! You should have seen their faces and then I couldn't get a word in edgeways."

"You mean you don't like Vlad?" Aunt Euphemia asked.

"No! At least not in *that* way. I've come to like him as a friend. Once you get beneath that arrogant exterior, he's actually quite a decent guy."

"I've found the same to be true," Aunt Loveday agreed.

"Oh my! You did give us a scare. The thought of having to put up with his interminable moaning about walking in the shadows set me off!"

I laughed. "I think that you gave yourselves a scare."

"Well ... you do have terrible taste in men, Livitha."

"Pascal was not that bad!"

"He was a philandering toad, dear."

"Literally!" Aunt Thomasin cackled.

I wanted to jump to Pascal's defence. Yes, he had been unfaithful, but he wasn't a bad person and he had been a good husband in many ways. Instead, I shook my head and waited for the cackling to stop. I still hadn't told them about my intuition regarding Martha and Vlad.

"So, anyway, now that we've established that I have the worst taste in men in the entire universe, can I tell you about Vlad?"

Four pairs of eyes fixed me in their gaze. "Go ahead," Aunt Loveday said.

"Well, I know that Vlad keeps going on about finding Mina, but what if he found her again and we helped him keep her this time. I just find it so odd that he keeps chasing her through the centuries only to find her and then lose her again.

"Perhaps it's part of the curse?" Aunt Loveday suggested. "Maybe he's caught in a virtual time-loop. Time keeps going forward, but history repeats itself."

"Is there any way to stop history repeating itself so that they can be together?"

"I'm not sure."

"I think Vlad likes the chase! Being immortal, life can get pretty dull at times. Finding her again could be his only motivation to keep going."

"Do you think so?" I hadn't considered that idea. "But surely he'd be far happier if he found her and she stayed with him—for eternity? I mean, he's so miserable without her."

"He's certainly boring about it."

"Shh! He may hear us, Thomasin. It would be unforgiveable for us to be so disrespectful to him whilst he is our guest."

"Oh, he's wrapped up warm in his snuggly wolf blanket, dead to the world in that box."

"He's certainly dead!"

Giggles, only half-suppressed, filled the kitchen.

"And I'm pretty sure," Aunt Thomasin continued, "it's insulated and sound-proofed."

"How do you know that? Have you been snooping down there?"

Aunt Thomasin responded with a shrug.

"Nevertheless," Aunt Loveday said with a disapproving shake of her head, "we should be careful with the choice of our words!"

"Well," said Aunt Euphemia, "I think the question is, why does she always disappear once he's found her?"

"Hmm!"

"I can list ten good reasons right now," Aunt Thomasin quipped.

"Oh, Thomasin!"

"Well, I have had quite enough of him banging around at night, slamming windows and doors and creaking across the floorboards. And then there is the continual complaints. Nothing is ever quite right, or hot enough, or cold enough. And if I hear about 'the shadows' one more time I may just scream!"

"Now, now, let's all be understanding. It can't be easy for a man to have to shackle himself to the dark hours. I would simply die inside if I weren't able to go out into the sunshine. Imagine never seeing the colour of flowers, or the sky, or fields of golden corn ever again!"

A communal murmur of sympathy.

"I suppose," Aunt Thomasin conceded.

"And it won't be too much longer before he leaves. I think he plans to travel home before the Autumn Equinox."

"Oh, yes! Hallowe'en will soon be here!"

"I can't wait."

The conversation was veering away and if I didn't step in then it would be lost for good. "Anyway, as I was saying, I think we should help Vlad and Mina."

"How on earth can we do that?"

"Well ... I think I've found her!"

"Never!"

"Yes!"

"How? Where is she?"

"Well," I said, "It struck me that Martha, the woman that owns the new shop-"

"Ooh! You didn't tell us about last night. How did it go?"

"Were many people there?"

"What does she sell?"

I was losing control of the conversation again! "It was ... different but let me tell you about Martha and Vlad first."

"Martha and Vlad?"

"Let me explain."

They nodded and I continued, describing Martha and my impression of her.

"She sounds interesting. But what has she to do with Vlad?"

"Well, don't you think it's odd that this mystery woman turned up when Vlad arrived? She has a Slavic accent like Vlad's too."

"Her name sounds Russian."

"Vlad isn't Russian."

"I know-"

"Vlad isn't particular where his brides come from. The one he beheaded was South African."

"Or Australian."

"Hmm."

"Well, he has been searching for Mina for centuries, so she's more likely to be of local-ish origin? So Russian kind of fits?"

"Perhaps."

"That makes sense although Vlad has always travelled widely."

"I thought he met Mina in Whitby?"

"Not originally, dear."

"Anyway," I said in an effort to steer the conversation again, "I think Martha may be the woman he's searching for. Her name is Martha, which is similar to Mina.

"Well ..."

"Rather tenuous, Livitha."

"I'm not sure that's a strong enough reason to suspect ..."

"There's more!" I insisted. "She also mentioned something to Dr. Cotta about being in a complicated relationship and searching for the man she loves!"

"I guess it's worth considering."

"But don't you think it's worth introducing them to each other ... just in case?" I suggested.

"I wouldn't interfere, Livitha," Aunt Loveday schooled.

"Fools do rush in, where angels fear to tread!"

"Precisely."

"Indeed."

"Well," said Aunt Loveday in a signal that the conversation was closed. "We really do have a lot of work to do today in preparation for tonight." She clapped her hands. "Chop, chop, sisters!"

On Loveday's command, the kitchen became a bustling hive of activity. I finished my breakfast and joined my aunts in making the final preparations for the opening but, despite their lack of enthusiasm for my conclusion, I was determined to dig a little further and discover if Martha was indeed Mina. Tonight's opening would give me the perfect opportunity. I was sure Martha would turn up at the shop. There was only one problem, I had already told Vlad to bring Mindy!

Chapter Eighteen

The afternoon was spent making sure the shop was ready for the opening that evening. I became increasingly on edge. I wanted Vlad and Martha/Mina to reunite but not at the shop. I knew that Vlad intended to come with Mindy in tow and thought that Martha would also turn up, even if it was just to check out the competition. I had to intervene.

Two hours before opening, with my aunts dressed and ready for the evening, I dropped them at the shop then returned to the cottage to speak to Vlad. Time was limited and, at the first hint of dusk I woke him. Again, there was no sign of Igor and I quickly lit the candles, placed Vlad's slippers at the side of the box then unclipped the locks. A muffled and annoyed grumble answered my insistent rapping knock.

"Vlad! It's Liv. Open up!"

The lid slid to the side revealing a deathly pale, slightly puffy-eyed, vampire.

"Where is Igor Nicolae Țăranu?"

"I'm not sure." I had a suspicion that he was with Martha but didn't elaborate.

Vlad grumbled, stated that Igor was an imbecile, a lazy turd with the social skills of a parsnip, and that he was glad he wasn't around to bore him to death, then threw his cosy wolf-print blanket to one side and sat bolt upright in a single slow movement.

Frustrated by his lack of any sense of urgency I urged him to be quick.

"Do not worry, Livitha. I will be at the opening of your shop. I am grateful for the invitation and honoured to be there."

"No! It's not that. There's someone I want you to meet before the shop opens."

"Who."

"I'd rather just show you. I think you may know them, but I won't know until you meet."

"This is intriguing. My life can be dull, so many years pass in dullness. I accept!"

Vlad dressed with impressive speed and we were soon motoring to the village. I was intrigued as to how the man had become the monster so used the time alone to ask a few personal questions.

"So, you becoming a vampire-"

"I am Dracula!" he snapped.

"Yes, sorry!"

"I should apologize. I am a grouch when I first rise."

"Understandable," I placated. "Do you mind if I ask you a few ... personal questions."

"It is so long since anyone showed interest – apart from Mindy of course – so yes, go ahead."

"Well ... so, you becoming Dracula ... immortal ... was it a curse? Because I've come across a lot of cursed people recently and there might be a way of getting it lifted."

"A curse? No, it was my own doing. I made a pact with the dark forces of the universe."

"Oh, well, perhaps-"

"I did it to find my Mina. She was my first bride, cruelly torn from me. I vowed to avenge her death. I vowed to find her again. But they mock me! It is a never-ending quest. I find her and she is taken again. In the meantime, I have my wives, but always, always I walk in the shadows and I look for her."

"Well ... if you did a deal with the 'dark forces' maybe you could renegotiate?"

"No! I must walk in the shadows for eternity," he said with dramatic flair.

"Well, yes, I get that, but the whole seeking Mina thing, perhaps there's a way for you to find her and keep her?"

He became thoughtful. "What do you suggest?"

"Well, my aunts know so much magick, perhaps they can intervene—cast a spell to keep her with you for eternity?"

"Do you really think it could work?"

"I think it's worth exploring."

He became silent then brooding.

We made it back to the village in record time and pulled up outside Martha's shop. It sat in darkness, but a light shone from the upstairs apartment.

I led him down a passageway and into the yard at the back of the shop. A steel staircase led to the apartment above.

"Where have you brought me, Livitha?" he asked as we stood at the bottom of the steps.

"Well," I said, barely able to suppress my excitement. "There's somebody I'd like you to meet. She's upstairs."

"She?"

"Yes. Come on."

Vlad stalled as I began to climb. "I am not sure about this."

I was about to cajole him when the door to the apartment opened and Martha, hidden by a hooded cloak, stood with her back to us as she locked the door. Tense moments passed as I watched the pair. Martha began to descend the steps oblivious to us as she focused on her mobile. Vlad stood at the base of the staircase with his eyes locked on the cloaked figure. His face was inscrutable but as Martha reached the last few steps and raised her head, his eyes widened. My heart raced as I waited for that moment of recognition.

Vlad hissed as though he were a pressure cooker letting off steam.

Martha/Mina stood speechless and then blurted "Vladimir!"

My heart skipped a beat. I had reunited Vlad with his soul-mate.

"You have come back to me!"

Vlad turned to me with a vicious scowl. An electric shot of fear raced along every nerve in my body as his eyes sparked red.

"Is this a joke, Livitha Erikson?"

"No!" I blurted realising something was terribly wrong. "I ... I found her for you, your Mina!"

Martha groaned, the smile on her face instantly dropped, her eyes narrowing to mirror Vlad's.

"Mina?" he shouted. "This is not Mina! This!" He jabbed a finger at the woman. "This ... creature," he spat, "is Martha Vasilevna Sobakina. The woman who I came here to avoid; my wife!"

Chapter Nineteen

I was dumbfounded and stood mute.

Vlad and Martha stood as statues as they glared at one another.

Igor appeared from the passageway but quickly retreated.

Vlad's eyes flashed red and he hissed, baring his fangs. Undaunted, Martha returned the scowl with a hiss of her own. Like two cats preparing to fight, they were on high alert, ready to attack at any moment.

Then Vlad's demeanour changed, and he took a step away from Martha and turned to leave. With a dismissive flick of his hand, he began to walk away.

"Hah! Walk away! It is what you always do."

Vlad spun back on his heels. "I have told you to leave me alone! Why must you always follow me?" He turned back to me with a pained expression. "Always she follows," he said. "Stalking me wherever I go! She is not right." He tapped at his temple, "up here!"

"And whose fault is that?" Martha spat.

Vlad groaned. "Here we go," he muttered.

I became a spectator in their marital spat as Martha rounded on the Count.

"I was just a trophy for you! You took me from my family. You stole me from my husband!"

He groaned. "Blah, blah, blah! It is always the same. You stole me from my husband. Five, four, three, two, one ..."

"I was the wife of Ivan the Terrible. I had a place in society. I was loved and adored, but you stole me from life."

"Are you listening to this, Livitha?"

I nodded. I was more than listening, I was fascinated.

"You murdered me just to add me to your collection of wives!"

A flicker of pain passed through the Count's eyes. "Martha, for three hundred years I have listened to you tell me about how wonderful Ivan was! The man was a monster! I rescued you!"

"I did not need rescuing!"

"I saved you, Martha!" Vlad turned to me. "She was dying! Her own mother fed her poison."

"Not on purpose!"

"To make her more fertile. Hah!"

"And I would have been fertile. I would have given Ivan many babies if you hadn't stolen me!"

"Not this again. Martha ... you were dying! I saved you. I gave you eternal life! You should be grateful."

"I was grateful for three hundred years and seventy-two days and then you threw me away! I gave you the best years and then you traded me in for a younger model."

He groaned and squeezed the bridge of his nose. "And for every one of those three hundred years and seventy-two days I tried to make it work!" He said this with emotion, and I sensed the depth of his pain. "But it just doesn't. You must accept this!"

"You never loved me!" she threw back at him. "Never."

"I love all my brides," he said softly.

"But you never *really* loved me!"

"I did my best to love you, but I have only one soulmate and she-."

Martha raised a hand. "No! Do not tell me. 'My Mina!'

"Yes! Always I walk through the shadows-."

"Seriously, Vlad! Are you still on about that! You sound like a stuck record. Mention the woman's name and out it comes, 'My Mina. Always I walk in the shadows in my eternal search for her soul!'"

Martha's impression of Vlad was spot on.

"Have you never asked why it is that she always disappears once you've found her? How many times is it now that you've walked through the shadows, found her, then lost her again?"

"Well ..."

"I'll tell you how many—seven! Seven times you've found your soul's mate and lost her once again."

"Well-."

"And just why do you think that is?"

"It is fate! I am damned to walk alone in the shadows!"

"No! It is not fate. It's because she just doesn't like you. She doesn't disappear! She runs away screaming."

"That is not true!" Anger flickered in his eyes. "My Mina ... she loves me!"

"My Mina! My Mina! My Mina!" I am sick of hearing that woman's name. "Give up chasing through the shadows, Vladimir Tepes! Come back to me!"

"It's over between us Martha. Go home."

"I will go home, but ... come with me!"

He groaned and his shoulders sagged. "The renovations will take a little longer."

"But then you will come home?"

"Perhaps."

My jaw dropped at this turn in the conversation.

"Do you still live with her?" I asked.

"I live with all of my brides," Vlad admitted. "Martha has a suite in the castle. One of the best suites!" he added with a meaningful glance at the beautiful woman.

"Oh."

"Yes, I am a stupid, soft-hearted man."

Martha reached out a hand. "Come home with me, Vladimir. The nights are lonely without you."

Vlad groaned then shook his head. "Martha," he said whilst holding her gaze. "I want a divorce."

For several moments the words seemed to have no impact and then she exploded into fury.

"No one rejects me!" she hissed.

"Here we go! Again!"

"No one rejects Martha Vasilevna Sobakina, the wife of Ivan the Terrible."

"It is always the same. 'I am the wife of Ivan the Terrible. How dare you, blah, blah, blah! Martha, you were married to him for four days!"

"Well ... they were four wonderful days!"

Vlad groaned. "I have heard this a thousand times! You fell sick before you married him. You could barely stand at the ceremony. You had been poisoned, Martha. You were dying!" He threw this at her as a plea. "I saved you from death!" Vlad threw his hands in the air as Martha began another barrage of accusations. "Enough! I have had enough. Go back home, Martha. We will talk there."

Without waiting for her response, he grabbed my elbow and led me to the passageway.

"I should have chopped her head off!" he grumbled as we emerged onto the path.

"I'm so sorry!" I exclaimed. "I had no idea she was your wife."

"I was so careful this time," he said. "I told no one where I was going, but still she found me. I can never get away from her!" He sighed. "Livitha! Take me to Mindy."

Chapter Twenty

After taking Vlad to Mindy's house, which was thankfully not far from the village, I arrived back at the shop with ten minutes to spare.

We opened at eight pm as planned, to a large group of villagers gathered outside. They clapped as Aunt Loveday unlocked the door and welcomed them in.

Inside, the shelves were stacked with jars and bottles of lotions, salves, moisturisers, bath oils, soaps, elixirs, and potions. The new shelves had been waxed, and the floor polished. An old glass-fronted haberdashery cabinet ran along the length of one wall and acted as a counter. Behind it were two renovated Welsh dressers that the builder-come-handyman, Mike, had painted black. I had been unsure of his choice of colour at first but was now pleased that I had agreed. His instinct was good, and the black worked well with the muted wooden tones of the shelves and the haberdashery counter. Black also helped to showcase our beautiful glass bottles and jars. In the middle of the shop was a central island with a marble top, a renovated piece, reclaimed from a large kitchen. Again, Mike had painted the base black. The multiple paned Georgian bow windows had been carefully restored with the rotting wood replaced and the whole frame stripped and repainted. Mike had gone to enormous lengths to make the shop ready for the opening and he had done a beautiful, top-quality job.

Warm light filled the shop. We had opted for warm white overhead lights rather than a stark white and this, along with the candles flickering in the silver wall sconces that Aunt Loveday had found in storage at the cottage, added a welcoming glow. The whole place was unique and quirky, and perfectly reflected Haligern Cottage and its secret coven.

Laughter and chatter filled the room. The three cakes I had made sat atop glass cake stands on the central island along with the bottles of wine, plates, and glasses. The kettle boiled in the back kitchen for any customers who preferred a cup of tea. In another storage room at the cottage, I had found a mismatched collection of prettily decorated teacups and saucers and these too sat on the central island beside a large teapot with a delicately tapered spout that I was sure dated to the late nineteenth century.

Customers trickled in and chatted happily with my aunts. When the bell rang on the till signalling our first sale, I wanted to clap, but restrained myself and instead beamed across at Aunt Loveday. With Uncle Raif at her side, the candlelight illuminating her silver cloud of hair with gold, she was the picture of elegance and radiated beauty. Together, their arms entwined behind the other's back, their love for each other, and the villagers they served, glowed. The atmosphere in the room was completely different to Martha's opening. There, I now realised, the chatter and laughter had been stilted and brittle, the people more interested in being seen, and seen to be amusing. Here the laughter was genuine, the chatter amiable and honest, the questions about the products sincere. The bell on the till rang again and happiness spread through me like a wave.

As darkness fell outside, the flow of customers continued, and Vlad, accompanied by Mindy from the Morgue walked in. His entrance was fairly low-key, at least for the Count, and he had chosen to wear dark blue denim jeans and a nicely aged tan leather jacket over a black t-shirt. He looked casual, attractive, and, as he ushered Mindy inside, happy, if not a little nervous. He seemed recovered from his earlier debacle with Martha.

I could see why he was attracted to Mindy. She looked to be about thirty years old and had a mass of auburn and curling hair that framed a sweetheart face. Freckles dotted her nose. Her makeup was minimal, but with her youthful complexion, honey-coloured skin, and dark lashes ringing green eyes the colour of emeralds, she didn't need it. Vlad clasped her hand as he caught my eye, waved, then made his way to the central island, poured her a drink of wine, and cut her a slice of cake. Together they made an attractive couple.

As the bell on the till rang again, three tall figures caught in the periphery of my vision as they entered the door. I turned to see Dr. Cotta waving across at me. Beside him stood the Reverend Parsivall and behind them both was Garrett. Flashlight made each blink as photographs of their entrance were taken. Both men continued into the shop, ignoring the man with the camera. I recognised him instantly as the journalist who had badgered us after the sinkhole incident; Keith Cleghorn from the Liarton Caller. Keith had been at Martha's opening too, and I had assumed he had been invited as part of her marketing efforts. Press attendance at our opening hadn't been part of my plan and I had realised my mistake as soon as I saw him at Martha's opening.

As Dr. Cotta and the Reverend walked towards me, Cleghorn continued to photograph them then turned his attention to Garrett. Lights flashed in his face, but he remained calm with only the slightest flicker of annoyance as he pushed past the journalist.

"Liv!" Dr. Cotta leant in, grasped my elbow, and placed a warm kiss of welcome on my cheek. I lost sight of Garrett as he, and the Reverend, blocked my view. "Looks like a bonza evening!"

"It's going well," I replied. "Can I get you some cake?" I motioned to the cakes and tortes sat on their gleaming glass stands. "A drink?" I cut two more slices from the rapidly disappearing cakes and poured two glasses of wine. Minutes passed as Dr. Cotta admired the shop and the Reverend Parsivall congratulated me on a successful open evening.

"Well, it's not as glamorous as Martha's, but it is going well."

"It's going great, Liv, and this cake is delicious!" Dr. Cotta said as he forked the last bite into his mouth.

"Can I get you another slice?"

"Well, I shouldn't but ... could I try ... no! I'd best not." He patted his waist. "It doesn't burn off as quick as it used to!"

"Tell me about it," I laughed.

"Why don't you have another slice, Parsivall? He never puts on an ounce. Isn't that right, Parsivall?"

The Reverend took a sip of wine, and smiled, his green eyes holding mine. "That's right, but I do run five miles on most days, so I guess that helps."

I cut him another slice.

Flashlight blinded me as I turned to hand him the plate. As my eyes adjusted, Keith Cleghorn's face appeared from behind a large camera. He scrutinised me for several seconds then turned his attention to a group of women inspecting salves and lotions. I noticed Garrett watching me from across the room. He quickly looked away when he caught my gaze. Heat began to rise in my core, my fingers tingled, sweat surfaced on my top lip. I had to cool down. Excusing myself, I walked to the back of the shop and stepped with relief into the open air.

Stars twinkled overhead and the cool night air held the promise of autumn. Having Dr. Cotta and Garrett in the same room made my nerves jangle. After just a few minutes, refreshed although still on edge, I returned to the shop and threw myself into talking to the customers and answering their questions. Under the guidance of my aunts, my knowledge of our products and their healing, therapeutic properties, had grown enormously over the last few weeks and I was pleasantly surprised at how helpful I could be. The evening progressed with a constant trickle of new customers and although the crowd thinned at times, the shop was never empty. Keith Cleghorn continued to take photographs and talk to the customers. I hoped his write-up would be favourable.

As I consulted with Aunt Euphemia on the best lotion for a customer who professed to have 'bone ache', Keith Cleghorn returned his attention to the Reverend and Dr. Cotta by taking numerous photographs of them. A frown settled on the Reverend's face and he exchanged words with Dr. Cotta who seemed to placate him. They both turned away from the journalist and his flashing camera. Undeterred, he took several more photographs pointing the lens at their feet. At this the Reverend Parsivall snapped and took a threatening step towards the man. Sensing the situation was about to turn into a fracas, I stepped in.

"Mr Cleghorn, if you continue to harass my customers, I'm going to have to ask you to leave." I was surprised at the commandeering tone in my voice.

Cleghorn raised a hand in submission and took a step back. "No offence intended," he said. "I'm just supporting local business."

"I appreciate that, but perhaps you could be a little less ... obvious whilst you work?" I said this in placatory tones whilst still trying to maintain my authority. To my surprise he flashed me a smile and made a comment about how well it was going. "My piece will be in tomorrow's paper. I hope it helps." He sounded genuine and, fter slipping between a group of customers, he began to photograph the displays.

Ten minutes later tempers flared again and this time my efforts at intervening failed!

The shop was effectively two rooms with steps leading up to the second at the back. I had convinced my aunts that we should sell products other than our own wares and the second room was stocked with items that could be bought as gifts. I had hung mirrors in the spaces between the dressers and shelving units that lined the walls, and soft light bounced from them.

To busy myself between customers' questions I tidied and re-stocked the shelves. In the back room Parsivall had cornered Mindy and they were deep in conversation. Vlad was in the main room pouring another glass of wine. Mindy worked at the funeral home as a morgue technician preparing bodies for burial and, as Parsivall owned the business, it wasn't unnatural that they should be talking. I edged closer, placing several new jars of salve on a depleted shelf. From Parsivall's body language I could tell that he was on edge. The laid-back demeanour of the man who had complimented me on my cake and cast an appreciative eye around the newly renovated shop, had transformed to a brittle energy. He was tense and towered over Mindy. I honed-in on their conversation, tuning in my new and improved witchy hearing.

"It's over!" Mindy hissed.

Parsivall grabbed her elbow. "It's only over when I say it is."

She tugged at his grip. "Get your hands off me!"

"Make me!"

Surprised at the venom and threat in his voice, I decided that it was time for me to intervene but as I took a step towards them, a figure pushed past me. The next moments were a blur as Vlad picked Parsivall up by the back of his jacket and held him aloft. Mindy tugged her arm from Parsivall's grip. Incessant clicks were accompanied by flashing light as Keith Cleghorn took multiple shots, following the action as though filming a scene from a movie. Vlad threw Parsivall to the floor. The Reverend stumbled then knocked into a shelving unit. Jars and bottles clinked as it shook. A bottle toppled then crashed to the floor. Its flower-infused and oily contents leaked. Mindy fled down the steps. Vlad followed. Garrett grabbed Cleghorn's collar and insisted he stop taking photographs. Cleghorn began to bleat about police oppression and freedom of the press. Dr. Cotta steadied the shelves as Parsivall attempted to stand but slipped in the oil and landed with a heavy thud. The lotions, potions, salves, and elixirs tinkled against each other.

My opening was crashing down around my ears, literally, and then Martha arrived.

Chapter Twenty-One

As Parsivall finally managed to stand, Martha appeared in the shop's doorway. Elegant in skinny jeans and crisp white shirt, her outfit was completed with high heels and a wide band of glittering diamonds at her neck. Glossy hair shone and the soft light gave her eyes a smoky look. Her beauty was marred only by the frown that fell across her face as she noticed Vlad with a consoling arm around Mindy's shoulder.

Suddenly the atmosphere in the shop changed. Even the temperature seemed to drop. Several customers made a hurried exit, clutching their jackets as though to ward off the cold. One made the sign of the cross and almost ran through the door and into the street. Others were oblivious and either continued to look at the products or were watching Dr. Parsivall's failed efforts to stand with the amusement of spectators at a circus.

Martha, her eyes locked to Vlad, strode across the room.

My fingers tingled.

The opening was descending into chaos. Fingers sparking, I gritted my teeth, pushed down the rising, maelstrom of energy, and also made a beeline for Vlad.

I managed to stand between the pair just as Martha opened her mouth to speak. Her jaws snapped shut as I blocked her way. Her brows pulled together in a deep frown and there was a definite red tinge to her eyes. It was then that I noticed her perfectly white and slightly too long incisors. The hairs on my neck stood on end.

You are a powerful witch, Liv. Deal with this! "Martha," I said as the tips of my fingers began to hurt. "I don't want any trouble. Please, this is our opening night."

Keith Cleghorn's camera flashed. It struck me then that Keith was going to be another thorn in my side. Not only was he becoming annoying to my guests, but now he was photographing Vlad and Martha, both vampires, both of whom wouldn't appear in the photographs. I batted a hand at Keith. "Please, Mr Cleghorn, no more photographs."

By now, the scene had my aunts' attention. All four were watching. How much of the debacle with Parsivall they had seen I wasn't certain but, with the crowd now thinning, we had become the centre of attention. I had to deal with this situation without causing a scene, or using my magick, or depleting the happy atmosphere that had pervaded the opening, any further.

Violet eyes locked onto mine and then with a slight curl on her perfectly painted lips, she dismissed me. With her high heels, she towered over me and scowled at Vlad.

"What are you doing with this woman?" she spat.

"It is nothing to do with you, Martha Vasilevna Sobakina."

"Hah! It has every-think to do with me, Vladimir Tepes."

"Can you at least take this outside, please?" I made an effort to be politely authoritative. They completely ignored me.

"Vlad," Mindy said, "who is this woman?"

"She is nobody, my dear. Ignore her." Vlad locked eyes with Martha. "She is a harridan, a nag, a psychotic stalker, and has the social manners of a turnip."

"A stalker?"

"Yes, she follows me wherever I go."

"Can't you call the police!"

"I am tired of running."

"A stalker, Vlad?" Anger flickered in Martha's eyes.

"Please!" I hissed. Several of the villagers were now watching the scene with interest. My aunts were exchanging worried glances. "This is not the place-"

"No! I am not a stalker," Martha said whilst flashing a gloating smirk at Vlad. "I am Vlad's wife!"

"His wife!" Mindy's eyes opened wide. "You never said you had a wife."

"We are separated." Vlad stated.

"But you never told me!" Mindy removed Vlad's arm from her shoulder. "You said you were single."

"I am single. This woman is nothing to me!"

Martha reared and launched into a tirade of accusations. Several more customers scurried from the shop. Still others stood mesmerised by the argument, obviously entertained.

My efforts to diffuse the situation failed and I could only watch as Martha accused Vlad of being unfaithful whilst he thew back at her that she was an interminable nag with the social grace and charm of a rotting turnip. He was surprisingly meek, or ineffective, against the woman's deluge of accusations, only baring his fangs in a hiss of anger when Martha unleashed her anger on Mindy.

A flicker of fear flashed in Martha's eyes and Mindy ran from the shop.

As she disappeared into the street and Vlad pushed past Martha to follow, three women hovered at the doorway blocking his exit. When I say hovered, I don't mean they were just lurking, I mean their feet were actually hovering above the ground. I recognised them instantly as the three women Vlad had disappeared with at Whitby. Still dressed in their hen-night regalia of shiny red sateen corsets and ballerina skirts of black nylon netting, they looked rough. A dog, a small and very furry white Pomeranian with glowing red eyes yapped at their feet. All thoughts of Mindy disappeared as I stared at the trio and their pet hellhound in horror.

"Oh, Vlad!" one called. "Are you coming out to play?"

The other two giggled. The dog yapped and snapped at the customers although it made no effort to enter the shop. Red stained the fur at its collar.

"It's a vampire dog!" I whispered then clamped my lips together.

The women floated at the doorway. Like the dog, they made no effort to come inside.

Martha cackled, then said, "So, you have been collecting even more brides. Hah! And from the state of them, it looks as though you are becoming desperate in your old age, Vladimir!"

"Vlad," I said turning to the vampire as the remaining customers huddled in groups. "These are the women from Whitby!"

"They are."

"But you promised!"

"I am sorry!"

"Deal with them, then! Get rid of them."

As Martha continued to laugh, Vlad scooped up the rabid Pomeranian and shooed the women away from the door. A collective sigh of relief filled the room. My aunts gazed from the doorway and then back to me. I had to do something to normalize the situation. I began to clap. All four aunts watched me, bewildered.

"Bravo!" I cried and clapped harder. Another clap joined mine. "That was an outstanding performance!" I continued to clap, catching the eyes of as many of the remaining customers as I could. "Martha, take a bow!" I hissed as more people joined in with my clapping.

"But-"

"Just do it, please!"

To my relief, Martha bowed. The claps became louder. I grew in confidence.

I took the bunch of flowers from the vase on the central island and handed them to Martha as though she were the leading lady in a play. As the clapping diminished, I thanked her for her outstanding performance, thanked the villagers for turning up to support our opening, and announced that the evening was about to end.

With the last customer gone, including Garrett and Dr. Cotta, I closed and locked the door, leaning back on it with relief.

"Well!"

All four aunts stared at me.

"That was ... not how I expected the evening to end."

"One thing is for sure; the village won't forget it in a hurry."

"You said you wanted to make an impact, Livitha, but I'm not sure that display will have quite the effect you wanted."

"The vampire dog was inspired! It added a definite touch of comedy to the scene."

As my aunts continued to churn over the chaos of the evening, I stepped outside for some fresh air. To my surprise

Vlad was already on the pavement. Smoke billowed around him as he took a drag on a cigarette.

"I didn't realise you smoked," I said. He took another drag. The tip glowed orange. Smoke billowed from his mouth. "It's bad for your health, you know."

"I am already dead, Livitha. How bad can it be!" He said this with a touch of bitterness.

"Sorry, I didn't mean to offend you."

"You didn't. It is I who must apologise. It is just ... just that being immortal ... there are so many things I cannot take pleasure in. Food – I cannot taste it. Wine – it has no effect. Smoking – nothing."

"Then why do you do it?"

"Habit. I started it to try and 'fit in.'"

"Well, people don't smoke so much nowadays."

He crushed the tab underfoot. "Pah! All these changes. I cannot keep up."

"Vlad ... where are those ... women?"

"At the cemetery. They are safe. You do not need to worry."

"It's hard not to."

"Martha, she is gone?"

"Yes. I think she went back to her apartment."

"Good. It is time I divorced her."

I mumbled in agreement, though uncertain what divorce meant to Vlad. The only ex-wife ever mentioned was the one he had beheaded. "Erm, do you think you could ... divorce her ... once you get back home?"

He grunted and was about to light another cigarette when a mobile phone rang. To my surprise, Vlad pulled a phone from his pocket, peered at the screen, then answered the call. He turned away, said, "I will be there," then turned back to me.

"Livitha, take me to the morgue. Mindy needs me."

Chapter Twenty-Two

The morgue, which was part of a funeral home, sat beside a cemetery which had its origins in the ancient past. A small church, built over a pagan temple, was situated at the far side of the cemetery and was largely unused, mourners now gravitating to the more modern building that also housed the crematorium. It was a fluid operation. Once certified dead, the body was brought to the morgue-cum-funeral home for preparation then held there until the day of cremation. Unlike many crematoriums and graveyards that had been hemmed in by housing and industrial estates, this one was situated in a semi-rural location to the east of the closest town and was surrounded by trees that thickened to woodland beyond the church.

Our journey took us up and through the hills where narrowing roads were overhung by trees and fog hovered above the ground making visibility low. As I rounded another bend, the car jolted and then bumped along, the steering suddenly heavy.

"What is it?"

"Sod's law!" I said with exasperation.

"Sod? Who is Sod?"

"Just a saying—if things can go wrong, they will!"

"Why are you slowing?"

"I have to. I've got a flat tyre."

"But I must get to Mindy!"

"I'll get you there, Count, but we have to fix this tyre."

"We? But I do not fix tyres."

I sighed.

"Call your friend. The policeman."

For once, I didn't want to call Garett. After tonight's exhibition of weirdness, he would ask far too many questions I would find it impossible to answer and I certainly couldn't tell the truth. "No. I can fix this, Vlad. I know what to do. And besides, if I call Garrett it will just take longer."

"How long will it take if you do it?"

"About twenty minutes?" I said popping the boot. I wasn't great with cars, but I did know how to change a tyre. It was the one thing that Pascal had insisted I learn, that and knowing how to check the oil and water levels.

"I cannot wait that long, Livitha! We will part company here. Do not wait up for me."

"I'm sorry but-"

The door slammed and, just as with our journey from Whitby, the Count disappeared into the fog.

This time I wasn't anxious; the Count knew his way back to Haligern. The only question was, if he had the power of transmogrification and flight, why had he bothered to ask me to take him to the morgue in the first place? I had to assume he just enjoyed being chauffeured or wanted my company.

It took at least twenty minutes to change the tyre and just as I re-started the engine and clicked the hazards off, headlights illuminated the fog. A car, going far too fast than was safe given the fog-bound and winding nature of the narrow road, hurtled towards me. I slammed the car into first gear, but the road was too narrow to move far. It wasn't far enough and, as I gripped the steering wheel, our wing mirrors clipped. All I saw was a flash of white. Despite the accident the car didn't stop. Angry and stunned I sat for several moments, relieved that only the wing mirror had been damaged, then drove to the nearest passing place, did a three-point turn, and returned to Haligern.

My aunts were gathered in the kitchen, drinking cocoa before they retired to bed. The last thing I wanted to do was dissect the failures of the evening so made an excuse to simultaneous murmurs of disappointment then made my way upstairs.

Lucifer lay curled on my bed and gave me a cursory glance before rolling onto his back and stretching out to fill as much space as possible.

"Lucifer!" I gave a tired sigh.

"Livitha!"

An attempt to pick the cat up and move it to the end of the bed resulted in the duvet rising as claws extended into the fabric.

"Lucifer!"

"Livitha!"

"Oh, for goodness sake! I'm tired. I've had a terrible evening."

"Worse than last night?" He asked, suddenly retracting his claws, and sitting to attention.

"Yes! Much. There was a fight and Vlad punched the Reverend Parsivall and then Martha showed up and accused him of being unfaithful. They made a terrible scene. Garrett saw it all!"

"Ooh! I should have been there. Sounds exciting."

I was a fool to expect Lucifer's sympathy. "I'm not sure exciting is the word I'd use, but that's not the worst of it."

Lucifer's eyes glittered. He stared at me as though I were a tasty morsel.

"You're loving this aren't you!"

"No! Of course not. Now, tell me. What happened next?"

"Well," I said slumping down on the bed. Lucifer bounced and toppled to his side, hissed something about a 'heffer' then jumped onto my knee.

"Tell me then!" he said with obvious impatience.

"Well, then three of Vlad's brides turned up and – and you're just not going to believe this – they brought their vampire dog with them."

Lucifer stiffened and yowled, digging his claws into my thighs. I yelped.

"A vampire dog!" he hissed.

"Yes, a vampire dog."

"Hideous!"

"Well, it was kind of cute, apart from the red eyes. I think it was a miniature Pomeranian."

"Unnatural! An abomination!"

"Says the talking cat!"

Lucifer hissed. "How very dare you!"

I leant back against the headboard, my eyes burning with tiredness. "Let's not argue tonight, Lou. I am absolutely shattered."

He huffed but remained on my lap, claws retracted. "Well, I suppose, but I want reparations in the morning!"

I was far too tired and overwrought to argue. "Port?"

"Yes."

"Salmon?"

"Yes."

"Deal."

"Good," he replied with satisfaction. "Now, I know that you're tired, but Vlad is at the window. Be a good girl and let him in."

As he finished, I heard tapping on the glass.

"I can hear a mouse at fifty paces, perhaps more," he said as I murmured in surprise. "And for goodness' sake, tell the man to use the door next time!"

"Right." I lifted Lucifer from my lap and placed him on the bed.

Behind the curtains, Vlad hovered at my window, his face, if it was possible, even paler than usual.

"Isn't your own window open?"

"I don't know. I didn't check."

"But-" I didn't finish the sentence, sensing that he wanted to talk and gestured for him to enter. "How did it go with Mindy?"

"It didn't." His morose tone matched the downward turn of his mouth. "She refused to see me."

"Refused to see you? But she was the one who called you and asked you to talk to her!"

"Yes, but when I got there, she did not answer the door."

"Were the lights on?"

"No."

"Well, perhaps she thought you weren't coming. A car passed me whilst I was changing the tyre, could that have been her? What colour car does she drive?"

"Red."

"Not her car then, but ... well, we weren't that long ... It's my fault, isn't it! If the car hadn't gotten a flat tyre she would have still been waiting!"

"It is not your fault that the car's tyre became flat—unless you used magick to make it flat?" He threw me an expectant, half-accusing, glance.

"No! Of course not. I wanted you to meet her—iron things out. She seemed like a nice woman."

"She was—is."

"Then call her. You have a mobile phone now ..."

"I tried, but there is no answer."

"Try again," I pestered.

As he pulled the phone out of his pocket to dial Mindy's number, scratching sounded at the window. The Count flinched and his eyes flitted to me. It was obvious he knew what was at the window.

"Leave it, Livitha. It is just a bat ..."

"Bat's use echo location. They wouldn't scratch at a window."

"A bird then."

The scratching repeated. I strode to the window and pulled the curtains open but dropped them quickly, gripping them shut. The three Goth brides hovered outside. "It's them!" I hissed.

Lucifer jumped off the bed and slunk beneath the curtains. "Ugh! I think you have visitors, Count. They had better not have brought their pet abomination along!"

Vlad pursed his lips.

"You gave us your word, Vlad! You promised to behave yourself."

"I have."

"You've ruined the shop's opening and vampires are infesting the village!

"My brides are not vermin!" the Count spat.

"No! Of course not, I didn't mean that! But you promised!"

"I have to see my Mina again. It was the only way I could think of to get her attention."

"But the women! You killed them!"

"I gave them immortality. Anyway, they were willing victims."

"They're Goth groupies, Vlad. It doesn't mean they wanted to become vampires."

"Of course it does. They are sycophants. It was their dream to become vampires, and I fulfilled their fantasies." He chuckled. "Now they are my beautiful Whitby Wives!"

The scratching continued. Vlad glanced at the window, obviously torn.

"Don't you dare invite them in!" I said as he began to pace the room.

"I won't," he said without conviction.

My head began to throb. If the women had been wandering around the village since Vlad arrived, it was no wonder that garlic was in short supply. It would also explain why there were rumours of strange goings on at the morgue. After tonight's appearance at the opening, the gossip would go into overdrive. "Vlad, you have to do something about them. They can't stay here. There isn't any garlic left in the village or the next town. People are getting anxious and we may be in the twentieth-century, but fear of witches and vampires is as real as ever."

"But they love us now!"

"It's a fascination fuelled by fear. There are many that want to see us eradicated." Memories of the men who chased me through the woods threatening to burn me and my aunts at the stake, was still raw.

Vlad continued to pace. Always it is the same, wherever I go the persecution begins!" he said with a frown. "They talk about accepting difference, but is it all just for show?"

"Well ... I guess people are more accepting these days, but ..." I wasn't sure what I could say, the general population was never going to accept the presence of a vampire who may or may not drink their blood and drag them into the realms of the undead. In that moment I had every sympathy with Vlad and could understand why he moaned about having to walk in the shadows for eternity.

The women scratched at the window again. Vlad sighed. "Excuse me, Livitha. My brides demand my attention."

Chapter Twenty-Three

The next morning, the chattering among my aunts lowered to whispers as I entered the kitchen. I poured myself a coffee and sat at the table, leaking disappointment.

Aunt Beatrice cut me a slice of bread and placed a pat of butter and a jar of homemade marmalade on the table. Aunt Thomasin busied herself sorting a pile of dried herbs, consulting a large and leatherbound tome then whispering ancient words as she tied them into bundles. Like Arthur, Aunt Loveday's book of spells and charms, this book was handmade and filled with quires of parchment. Writing and symbols in black ink crammed each leaf. Once the opening was over, my aunts had promised to begin my instruction and I was looking forward to creating my own grimoire. It was only when Aunt Euphemia returned from milking Olde Mawde that the silence was broken.

"Good morning, Livitha. I hope you slept well?"

I swallowed a mouthful of bread and marmalade. "Not too bad, thanks. Weird dreams, but nothing unusual."

"I'm not surprised. Last night was quite a ... surprise!"

Both Aunt Beatrice and Thomasin began to speak at the same time.

"It was eventful!"

"It was certainly memorable!"

"It was an opening that won't be forgotten any time soon!"

"I'm not sure your ... vampire stunt had the desired effect though."

"It wasn't a stunt!" I said.

"What would you call it then? A play? A drama?"

"It was certainly dramatic!"

"It was inspired, but I'm not sure it fits our ... do they call it branding? Whatever, it doesn't really fit how we want to be seen in the village."

"Exactly, it added an element of horror to the evening that will perhaps ... scare off the customers."

"That dog was something else. How did you get its eyes to shine red like that?"

"It was white, perhaps it was an albino. They have red eyes."

"It was a vampire dog!" I said, my head a whirl of thoughts. "And I didn't arrange any of it!"

My words unheard, they continued to chatter.

"Was it an improv troupe? That's what they call those, isn't it—where groups of actors just pop up and start acting?"

"No! I had nothing to do with it, those women just turned up. They're Vlad's brides," I admitted. "He met them at Whitby, before I arrived to collect him."

"But he promised!"

"He said he would behave himself!"

"He obviously didn't."

"Are you telling us that those women were vampires? And the dog too?"

"Yes, I'm afraid so."

"But how did you get them to join in the play, dear?"

"I didn't. It wasn't a play, or a drama, or an improv. I just said that to make the whole ... chaotic mess ... seem as though it was!"

The room grew silent for a moment.

"So, Martha really is Vlad's wife?"

"Yes!"

"This is a catastrophe!"

"Remain calm, Beatrice," Aunt Thomasin chided as sparks began to flash around Aunt Beatrice's aura.

"I'm not sure that I can, dear. We have an infestation of vampires in the village!"

"Loveday will know what to do."

Aunt Thomasin chuckled. "So, what do you call a vampire dog then?"

"It was a Pomeranian, so perhaps a vampom?" Aunt Euphemia suggested.

"More like a hellhound!" Aunt Loveday quipped as she entered the room.

Emotion welled up as she caught my eyes. Disappointment flickered there. "I am so sorry, Aunt Loveday," I said as she sat at the table. Aunt Thomasin pushed aside the bundles of herbs and closed her book. Aunt Beatrice prepared a pot of tea and Euphemia joined us at the table.

"What happened last night, Livitha? Everything was going so well. I don't understand how it all fell apart."

We pieced together the events from the evening. As far as I was aware, it was the Reverend Parsivall's less than friendly conversation that had kicked it all off. Vlad had come to Mindy's defence, but it wasn't until Martha had arrived that the evening had been ruined. The women turning up with the dog had rocketed it into a freakshow.

"Do you think they believed me, that it was all a show, a publicity stunt?"

"I'm not sure. It was certainly believable, but those women and that dog were rather terrifying."

"Where are Vlad's brides, by the way. Where is he keeping them?"

"At the cemetery."

Aunt Beatrice placed a large teapot at the centre of the table. "I'll be mother," Aunt Euphemia stated and set five cups and saucers in a row.

"Ah, no wonder there are rumours around the village."

"It explains the sudden interest in buying garlic too. It's obvious they haven't kept a low profile."

"I think they've been very restrained—in the circumstances. Newly turned vampires can be absolutely terrible to keep under control. Or so I hear."

"Like herding cats," Aunt Beatrice agreed. "Vlad must be keeping them under some sort of control. We would have heard of them sooner, if not."

"If turning a dog into a vampire could be seen as keeping them under control!"

"Well, there haven't been any reports of people rising from the dead."

Aunt Euphemia shuddered. "I do hope that he has plans to leave very soon."

"Perhaps he could be convinced to cut his stay short?" Aunt Loveday suggested.

"I think that he must. We simply can't allow the situation to escalate. Look what happened to the girls in Salem. They still haven't recovered from his visit."

Aunt Thomasin sipped her tea, then said, "Hmm, it was rather shocking."

"Well, we certainly have to take action."

"What do you suggest?"

Aunt Loveday was about to speak when someone knocked at the front door. "I'll get it," she said and disappeared from the kitchen.

"Who can that be?"

"I'm not sure," Aunt Euphemia said with a smile. "I have many talents but seeing through walls isn't one of them!"

"I bet it's that awful reporter. What was his name?"

"Keith Cleghorn," I answered.

A man's voice could be heard answering Aunt Loveday's enquiries and my stomach churned. It was Garrett. I brushed crumbs from my fleece and flicked at my hair, heart suddenly palpitating. The door closed and Aunt Loveday returned to the kitchen.

"Livitha," Aunt Loveday swept back into the room, her energy crackling. "DCI Blackwood wants to talk to you—on police business."

"Again!"

"Yes, again," she said with an air of disapproval. "They're waiting for you in the garden."

"They?"

Chapter Twenty-Four

G arret stood beneath the great oak, his back to me. At over six-foot with broad, muscular shoulders, and an only slightly thickening waist, I couldn't help admire his physique despite the rapid thudding of my pulse and the queasy sensation in the pit of my stomach. I was a child being summoned to the Headmaster's office.

He turned as I made my final approach. Our eyes met, but there was no welcoming smile. The churning in my gut intensified.

"Liv," he said without enthusiasm.

"Garrett," I replied noticing the redness in his eyes and stubble on his chin. He looked tired and a little unkempt. His shirt was crumpled, his hair uncombed.

A tall blonde woman dressed in similar style – dark slacks, blue shirt with the sleeves rolled up to her forearms - rather hairy forearms! - and sensible navy shoes stepped out from behind the great oak. On her lapel was a badge printed with 'PC W. Harker'.

I hid my surprise as Garrett pushed a hand through his hair, then, hands on hips said, "Liv, this is my partner. PC Harker."

PC Harker was surprisingly manly. At least five foot eleven, if not six foot, with broad shoulders, well-muscled arms, and thighs that bulged against her police issue trousers. It was obvious that she was athletic, and her waist was enviably slim although I noticed a slight growth of fine hair along her top lip. She wasn't unattractive but with heavy eyebrows and a slightly too large nose, I couldn't call her pretty. She also had a large mole just at the corner of her mouth, too big to pretend was a beauty spot. I know that it was uncharitable of me, but I felt a small skip of joy when I noticed several wiry hairs on her chin.

My heart thudded and my hands began to fizz. I clasped them together, pressing at my fingers in an effort to control the rising energy, telling myself that I was calm and in control. I took a breath, then said, "How can I help you?"

"We're here on police business, Miss Erikson," PC Harker replied. "We'd like to question you about your activities last night."

Here it was—the official investigation into the fracas at the opening. Had Parsivall pressed charges against Vlad? "I wasn't aware that people arguing had become a crime. No one was hurt, not really, and the ... violence was quickly gotten under control."

A confused frown descended on both their faces.

"Violence?"

"Yes, the fight at the apothecary shop. Reverend Parsivall and ... another customer came to blows."

Garrett shook his head.

"That's not what you mean?" My thoughts went to the Whitby Wives and their abominable Pomeranian x vampire mutt. "Oh, the other thing! Well, that was just a stunt. I know it's a bit until Hallowe'en, but I wanted to give them a trial and ..." Again, Garrett shook his head. PC Harker held me in her gaze as though I were a particularly interesting patient exhibiting strange behaviours. "Oh, well if it's not that, then what can I help you with?" I asked with increasing consternation.

"A woman has been murdered."

"Oh!"

"Where were you last night, Miss Erikson?"

Not again! "Last night?" I stalled, my thoughts a jumble.

"Yes, last night, after the opening. Where did you go?"

"I ... Who has been murdered?"

Garrett consulted a small notebook. "Miranda Cuthbertson."

"And the poor woman has been murdered?"

Both police officers nodded.

"I don't understand. I've never heard of Miranda Cuthbertson. Why do you need to question me about her murder?"

"She was a guest at your opening."

"Oh, well, there were a lot of people there last night, but I'll help where I can."

"Thank you," PC Harker said. "Miss Erikson," she continued. "We'd like to know your whereabouts after the opening."

"I ..." It dawned on me then. I had taken Vlad to the morgue to meet Mindy. "I went for a drive."

Garrett's face clouded over.

"Miss Erikson, where exactly did you drive to?"

"Well, just around. The evening had turned into a fiasco and I just needed to get away. I was upset."

"Upset? So, you admit that you were in an emotional state?"

"Yes."

"And perhaps you wanted to confront someone? Someone you blamed for causing the opening to fail?"

I had been angry and had wanted to confront Vlad. "I guess so, but what has this got to do with the woman who was murdered?"

"Liv ... Miss Erikson." Garrett swallowed. "We have reason to believe that you were in the vicinity when the woman was killed."

"What? But ... are you accusing me of murder?"

"No-"

"Not at this point in our enquiries," PC Harker stated.

"What? This is ridiculous. I haven't murdered anyone. I don't even know who Miranda Cuthbert is ... or was!"

"You may know her as Mindy. She was found this morning at her place of work. She had been dead for several hours."

"Mindy's dead!"

"She is."

"I can't believe it. She was at the opening. Vlad went up to meet her!"

"Vlad?"

I clamped my lips shut.

"Miss Erikson, if you have information that could further our enquiries you are obliged to tell us."

My head swam. Vlad had insisted that Mindy hadn't been at the morgue.

"There's something else," Garrett said. He watched me closely. "Miss Cuthbertson had puncture wounds on her neck and had been drained of blood."

Vlad did it! "That's ... that's horrifying!"

Thoughts scrambled as I failed to think of a good reason why I had been there without implicating myself further. Vlad had killed Mindy, or rather bitten her so that she could become another wife!

"Liv, your car was seen on the road to the cemetery, around the time when she was attacked. Can you explain what you were doing there?"

How on earth could I explain this without giving Vlad away? Haligern coven would be brought into disrepute! "You can't think that it was me!"

"As we said, you were seen close to the scene of the crime-"

"But that's insane, I would never ... could never kill some-one."

"Not even if they ruined your precious opening?"

"Are you sure she's actually dead?"

PC Harker's eyes narrowed. Garrett's frown deepened.

"There is no question about that."

PC Harker continued to stare at me. "We also need to question the man she arrived with at the opening." She described Vlad. "We believe that he is your house guest."

"Oh ... him. No, I mean he was, but he left a while ago."

"But he's still in the area?"

"Yes, I think so, well he's close enough to visit ... I guess. He was at the opening ... so ..." I was rambling, coming unstuck. I couldn't let them think that Vlad had anything to do with Mindy's 'death'. Regret that my aunts had ever accepted his request to stay suffused every cell in my body.

"I'm just going to talk to Miss Erikson privately for a moment, PC Harker. If you'll excuse us?" Garrett took my arm and walked me away from PC Harker then pulled out a mobile phone.

"Why is it when there's a murder, the trail leads back to you, Liv?" he said scrolling through the photographs. "I took these last night. Take a look and tell me what you see."

I leant in. In a photograph of the opening, I could be seen talking with Dr. Cotta. Mindy was there too but, where Vlad should have been standing, there was an empty space. Garrett showed me several similar photographs. Most damning of all though were a series where the Reverend Parsivall seemed to hover before being thrown across the room by an invisible force.

"They're interesting," was my lame reaction.

"Liv, the passenger in your car on the night I brought you petrol, is the same man who attended the opening last night. He arrived with Mindy. He also punched the Reverend Parsivall, who seemed to be arguing with the victim. I saw him, with my own eyes, but he's not in these photographs."

"Maybe a faulty camera? Have they been edited?"

"Liv, you were seen leaving the shop with him and getting into your car and then travelling in the direction of the morgue."

"It's not a crime to go for a drive!"

Garrett sighed. "Her blood was drained. There were two puncture wounds to her neck. Liv, I know this is going to sound crazy, and I think you may just be the only person around here who might not think so, but is Vlad a vampire?"

"No! That would be insane. Do they even exist?"

Garret grabbed my arm, "Liv, I know that you know more than you're telling me, but I think you and your aunts are in terrible danger."

"No, I'm sure we're not. Vlad promised to behave and anyway we're immune-" I had said too much!

"Immune? You think you're immune from a madman? What are you playing at, Liv?"

"Nothing!"

"He's a vampire!"

"He's a—was a guest."

"You're in danger, Liv! We have to find this man!" Garrett held my gaze. "Tell me where he is."

"I don't know," I lied.

PC Harker stepped beside us. "We need to speak to him, Miss Erikson, as a matter of urgency. Until we do, we cannot rule you out as a suspect. Your car was seen leaving the area and we have reason to believe there is probable cause."

Garrett shook his head. "Come to the station this evening, Miss Erikson. We need your official statement."

Chapter Twenty-Five

The kitchen was unnaturally quiet as I returned to my aunts. Each stopped their activity in expectation as I walked back through the door. Energy crackled and I left the door open to allow sunlight to flood in.

There was no point elaborating the point, so I put it bluntly. "A woman was killed last night, and they think Vlad is the murderer. I told them that he is no longer staying with us."

Worried glances were exchanged but no one denied that such an act by Vlad was impossible. Instead, Aunt Loveday asked if the unfortunate woman was someone we knew.

"Mindy," I replied. "The woman he was dating."

"The one he brought to the opening last night?"

"Yes."

"And she's dead?"

"Yes. They found her drained of blood at the morgue."

"Well, perhaps she's not dead in the traditional sense?" Aunt Thomasin said to murmured agreement.

"It sounds as if he has taken another bride," Aunt Euphemia said with authority. "I knew this would end badly! As soon as that invitation came through, I knew it. I said so. I did say!"

Aunt Loveday gave an exasperated sigh. "Well, it wasn't something we could refuse!"

"How many wives does the man want?" Aunt Thomasin exclaimed.

"Well, I am appalled at his lack of consideration. He said that he would behave himself whilst he was here. He promised to show us respect!"

"Hah! We were fools to trust a vampire."

"What will we do?"

"He has to leave. This is the last straw!"

"So, is she really dead?"

"If Vlad has bitten her then yes, and no! I guess he was ready to make her a wife."

"So selfish!"

"He's certainly only thinking of himself."

"And he promised! I will never trust a vampire again. Never!"

"What happened to a man being innocent until proven guilty?" I asked. Each of my aunts had instantly believed that he had killed the woman, as had I. "He should at least get the opportunity to defend himself before he is judged."

"Well ... the woman was drained of blood and he *is* a vampire, Livitha."

"That's true, but he's not the only vampire in the village at the moment," I said in his defence.

Murmured agreement was followed by expressions of concern for the coven's reputation.

"We should not have accepted the request for succour," Aunt Thomasin said with certainty.

"The Council would not look favourably upon that and don't forget how influential he is with the dark realm," Aunt Loveday said. "One day we may need him."

"Oh, fiddlesticks!" Aunt Thomasin returned. "It's time we looked for other allies. Vlad is only dragging us into disrepute."

"Shh! He may hear us," Aunt Beatrice scolded.

"Quite frankly, sister, I'm not sure that I care anymore. The village has become infested with vampires since his arrival. It was only a matter of time before disaster befell us."

The energy became increasingly fractious and embers sparked around my aunts' auras, each one crackling.

My next statement only added to their consternation. "The police think I'm involved."

Aunt Beatrice slumped into a chair. "Oh, Liv! Why?"

"Because I drove him up there last night. Mindy wanted to see him after the fight at the shop."

"That is the last straw. I demand that he leaves." Aunt Thomasin said with determination. "Livitha, telephone the shipping company and book him passage home on the Demeter, or any other ship that is available. Vlad must return home—with his wives!"

"And the dog!"

"Yes, and the dog."

"In the meantime, sisters," Aunt Loveday said with a grim countenance. "We must ensure that the authorities do not find him. We will never live this down if he is found at the cottage. The ramifications are unthinkable."

"I'll talk to him," I said glancing at my watch. It was only ten thirty in the morning, twilight was hours away.

"Don't wait," Aunt Beatrice said. "Wake him now. There's no sunlight in the cellar."

"We must have the truth, Livitha, and he must understand the need to leave Haligern but be careful how you broach the subject."

"Cast a protective spell, Loveday. Just in case."

"Just in case?"

"Yes. You know his reputation. He's a dangerous man—when crossed."

I swallowed, suddenly nervous about confronting Vlad. Asking the Count to leave the cottage was an insult and I had no idea how he would react, despite the friendship that had grown between us.

The entrance to the cellar was via a door beneath the stairs and I opened it with dread seeping down to my toes. Torchlight in hand, and a box of matches in my pocket, I descended the stairs. The scent of men's cologne hung in the cool and musty air. Vlad's box, which resembled a generously sized coffin, sat on trestles in the centre of the cellar. Candles in ornate candlesticks and candelabra were placed around the room and I lit each one before turning to the box. Even with the torch and the candles lit, darkness seemed to soak up the light. I flicked my hand, igniting my energy. A tiny ball of light grew until a hovering globe filled my palm and the brightness of my magick pushed back the dark shadows into the corners of the room. The brass clasps that secured the lid of Vlad's box glimmered in the light. I left them in the locked position and knocked on the box. Vlad grumbled but didn't stir. I knocked again.

"Vlad! It's me. Wake up!"

More grumbles. I waited for several moments, but when Vlad remained asleep, I knocked harder. "Vlad! I need to talk to you. The police have been here this morning. It's about Mindy."

This was followed by grunting then banging against the box's lid.

"Do you promise to stay calm?"

A muffled but irritated 'Yes!' filtered through the box.

With the clasps opened, the lid slid off and Vlad sat bolt upright in one fluid movement. I restrained a shudder. I had come to like Vlad, seen that he was a deeply troubled and complex man, but I would never see the way he sat up in bed as anything other than creepy!

"What time is it, Livitha? I do not feel refreshed."

"It's still daylight."

He shuddered. "Then it must be very serious this thing you want to talk to me about."

I took a stern tone. "It is. It's about Mindy."

"My Mindy? Is she here? What has happened?"

"No, of course she's not here. It's daylight and the last I heard she was laying dead at the morgue."

With that he clambered out of the box. "What?" He grabbed my arm. It lit up like an electric eel and, jerking with the current, he stumbled backwards.

"Sorry!" I said as he recovered. "It's just a precaution. We didn't know how you'd take the news."

He grunted. "Tell me that again! What has happened to Mindy?"

"You know what has happened, Vlad. What's important now is that we deal with it. The reputation of the coven is at stake. We have lived in peaceful harmony for centuries at Haligern, but now that the village has become – I was going to say infested, but quickly bit back my words – now that there are several vampires in the village, the situation has become ... untenable."

"Situation? Liv, stop talking in riddles. Tell me! What has happened to Mindy?"

I peered at him through suspicious eyes. "Well," I said whilst watching him closely. "She was found at the morgue. Her blood had been drained and there were puncture wounds on her neck. Everything points to a vampire's kiss!"

The Count swayed then staggered. I caught hold of his arm to help steady him. Electricity passed between us and he was jolted again, this time falling against the wall and hitting his head against the bricks.

"Sorry!" I gasped.

"Get back!" he hissed as I took an instinctive step towards him and held out a helping hand. "Are you trying to kill me!"

"Sorry!" This wasn't going the way I had expected. In my mind, I had confronted Vlad, and, after a few moments of denial, he had apologised and agreed to return home a little earlier than planned on the Demeter III or any other boat I could charter. Now, I had caused insult and injury too. "Sorry!" I repeated.

"Livitha, start from the beginning. You must tell me everything."

For the next minutes I explained about the visit from the police officers. Mindy had been found exsanguinated at the morgue and we were both prime suspects in her murder. "But, if she was bitten, if you had given her a 'love bite' – this was the term Vlad himself used when talking about transforming a living girlfriend into an undead bride – then she hasn't really been murdered-"

"Well, technically she has. Murder is the taking of life ..."

"Yes, okay, technically it is, but if she agreed to it, it's not quite murder, I guess."

"No, it is. In any court of law, it is murder, or at least manslaughter."

"Okay, well, you murdered her, but she will become one of your brides and ... undead, which is a kind of life ..."

"That is true, Liv, but I did not bite her. Last night, she would not answer my call. The lights were out at the morgue. I could not see her car. She was not there so I returned here."

A pall of dread fell over me. "So ... you didn't see her?"

"No! This I have told you many times."

"Then she really is dead? I presumed it was you and that you had bitten her to make her your wife?"

"No. We were dating. I wanted it to be different."

"But she was drained of blood. Garrett said there were puncture wounds on her neck, and she had been exsanguinated. So, if it wasn't you, then who?"

"Martha!" he blurted. "If Mindy was drained of blood, then it had to be another vampire. Martha is a vindictive woman. She has stolen her from me!"

"But when she wakes up, I'm sure she'll still want you."

"No. It does not work like that. Mindy has been stolen from me." He strode across the room and began to ascend the stairs.

"Vlad, no! It's still daylight."

He growled and stamped back down. "This living in the dark forever is a curse! I am a prisoner of the sun!"

As voices filtered down from upstairs, I had an idea. "Vlad, if you promise to stay calm, I can ask my aunts to come down here. We can figure this thing out together, but we can't have any more ... drama in the village!"

He grunted. "I will wait until sunset." He cocked his head to the stairs and a man's voice. "If that is Igor, I want him down here now."

Chapter Twenty-Six

Waiting for sunset seemed interminable and I busied myself in the garden for an hour before visiting the shop. We had planned to open today, but the turn of events had forced us to remain closed and I put a sign up that we were to open the following week. It took several hours to clean the shop and return it to a pristine state. Thankfully, the spilt oil cleaned up without staining the floorboards. My aunts had cleared away the cakes and took them home, but the pots remained to be washed. After cleaning away the debris of the party, I re-stacked the shelves, checked the inventory, and made a note of which items we needed to restock. By the time I was satisfied that I had done all I could for that day it was after five pm and I returned to the cottage on edge. The hours until Vlad could safely come out of the cellar had passed with difficulty but had also brought the time when I was expected at the station to give my statement far too quickly.

Stars were bright in a dark sky when Vlad finally arrived in a kitchen bristling with the fractious energy of five slighted witches. Already offended by the appearance of Vlad's Gothic Whitby Wives, my aunts weren't convinced of his innocence. Oblivious to the atmosphere, he waited beside the table as Igor pulled out a chair.

"My Mindy has been stolen from me! She was my bright star, guiding me as I searched for my Mina!" He gave a dramatic sigh.

"Here we go again," Igor huffed under his breath.

"I'm expected at the police station soon, we need to talk about my statement," I suggested.

Ignoring me, Vlad threw Igor a scowl then flicked a dismissive hand. "What would you know, Igor Nicolae Ţăranu? You are a peasant! You have never loved the way I have loved!"

"And whose fault is that!" he huffed.

"Are you accusing me of something?"

"Yes, I am! If it weren't for you, I would be with my Irena. She was my true love, but you took her from me."

"Hah!" The Count rounded on the old man now. "You lost her in a game of cards!"

"You tricked me!" Igor spat, straightening his back as far as his hunch would allow. "You tricked me! And you never kept your promise!"

"This again! I never promised to make you immortal."

"You did. I have it in writing." He pulled out a scroll of parchment. The letters, faded with time, were almost invisible. At the click of Vlad's fingers, the parchment crumbled to dust.

"Writing? What writing?" Vlad scoffed.

"That's not fair!" I managed and instantly pressed my lips shut. The tension in the room was palpable and it was obvious that the Count was far from stable.

"It doesn't matter!" Igor spat. "I'm going to be immortal anyway."

"Pah! And just how is that going to happen?"

"Never mind!"

"How!"

"Someone else has promised it to me."

"Someone else!"

"Yes, someone else."

"Man or woman?" Vlad demanded. "Tell me!"

"No."

"It's Martha, isn't it!"

Igor's eyes flitted to the side. "No!"

"It is! I saw you flinch."

"Well ... what if it is!"

"Pah! I'll tell you what if it is ... she's a liar." Vlad pressed his lips together, his eyes narrowing to slits. "It was you!" He jabbed a chunky finger at Igor. "It was you who told her where I was. After everything I have been through! You knew that I needed this holiday to escape her nagging and whining! But still you betrayed me! The woman is a psychotic stalker ..." His brows knitted together. "It has to be her! She is the one who took my Mindy!"

With uncharacteristic antagonism, Aunt Beatrice slapped her hand on the table. "And just how do you expect us to believe you, Vladimir Tepes?"

The Count looked taken aback.

"You've done nothing but deceive us since you arrived. The village is in uproar. There's no garlic left even in the next town, and our reputation is being dragged through the mud!"

"Well ... I did not do it!"

Aunt Beatrice huffed whilst my aunts looked on with a mixture of surprise and trepidation.

"I suppose Martha is a likely suspect," I said.

"Well, one of them did it!" Aunt Thomasin accused.

"What about his Whitby Wives?" Aunt Euphemia said. All the aunts seeped a belligerent energy. "Maybe it was one of them?"

Any concern about offending Vlad deserted, Aunt Thomasin said, "If it is, it's still Vlad's fault."

"No!" Vlad snapped back. "They are too young. It had to be Martha. I can prove it wasn't me."

"It's still your fault," Aunt Thomasin grumbled. "If you hadn't been here, neither would she!"

"Thomasin!" Aunt Loveday scolded. "I think you've gone too far with that comment."

Aunt Thomasin, arms folded in a defensive pose, pursed her lips.

"She is right. It is my fault. I can only apologise. I did not mean to bring catastrophe to you. I have been happy here."

"Thank you, Count," Aunt Loveday accepted with grace. "Now, we must figure out what to do. You said that you could prove that it wasn't you. Tell me how."

"We wait."

"How exactly will waiting prove that you didn't kill her," Aunt Thomasin asked, still resentful.

"She was drained of blood."

"She was."

"Well, if a vampire bit her she will rise from her grave and speak."

"I don't think she's in a grave," I clarified.

"Then where?"

"Well, I imagine in a chiller—at the morgue."

"Yes, yes, of course," Vlad agreed. "They must do the autopsy first."

"I guess."

"It is so. When a person is murdered, an autopsy must be carried out to determine the cause of death."

I was impressed by his knowledge. "You know a lot about the procedures."

"I have watched a lot of television. There are so many hours to fill. NCIS was one of my favourite shows—back in the day. So, Livitha, we must go to the morgue and wait."

"We!" I shuddered. "You're suggesting we interview a dead woman?"

"Technically, she will have joined the realms of the un-dead." He sighed. "But yes! Mindy, once she has woken, will tell us the truth of her death."

To my horror, Aunt Loveday agreed that this was a sound plan and instructed me to accompany Vlad to visit Mindy in the morgue and wait for her to rise from the dead.

Chapter Twenty-Seven

The drive to the morgue was accompanied by the obligatory rolling fog. My headlights illuminated the low-lying mist in a haze that only added to the creepy atmosphere. I gripped the steering wheel as my fingers crackled. So far, I was pleased with how well I had managed to subdue the unruly energy that wanted to burst from my hands. Igniting the witch light released the build-up of energy and gave me a sense of relief from the chaotic power and, in quieter moments over the past days, I had practiced using it. Now, driving along with Vlad on the way to watch a woman rise from the dead, anxious energy building, I was desperate for that relief.

We pulled up to the gates. They were locked and, to my surprise, Vlad jumped out of the car before I had a chance to suggest I use my magick to unlock them, tore the chain apart, and forced the gates open. I drove through and parked in a space overhung by trees. In all my imaginings of how my new magick-enhanced life would be, I had never considered that I would be waiting for a vampire to rise from the dead to give evidence against their killer.

As soon as I left the car, I lit my witch light. The relief from the pent-up energy and prickling in my hands was immediate.

"We should go around the back," I said as Vlad strode to the front doors. "We're breaking in. There could be guards on patrol." I scanned the area, but thick fog was rolling in at an unusually quick speed. I noticed the concentration on Vlad's face and the beckoning movement of his hands; he was bringing in the fog! "Are you doing that?" He nodded. "Very impressive!" I said with admiration. "Could you teach me how to do it?"

"No," was his abrupt reply. "My power comes from a different source. My methods would not work for you."

"Right, well, it's pretty amazing," I said in awe as the fog thickened. I made a mental note to search for a spell that would give me control over mist; it would be a fabulous first spell to include in my own grimoire.

"Come along, Livitha." Vlad waited beside the entrance. "The doors are locked. It is your turn."

Since my initiation, my aunts had waited to begin serious instruction to hone my growing powers, so my knowledge of spells was almost non-existent. However, I was learning to channel the primitive, unrefined magick at my core. I focused on the door, willing the ancestral voices to speak, but my efforts were met by silence.

"Are you alright? You look to be in pain."

"Give me a minute." I tried again.

Whispering voices began to rise.

"We haven't got all night, Livitha. The shroud of fog will not last and Mindy's reawakening will happen very soon."

Interrupted, the voices receded as I lost my concentration.

"I have to be with her when she does," Vlad continued. "I cannot bear the thought of her waking to a steel coffin, scared and lonely! Come along! Open the door," he nagged.

"Please," I said exasperated as the voices grew silent. "I need to focus."

"Go ahead! But hurry!"

I will if you stop nagging! Palm flat against the door, I called on the ancient magick of my ancestors. With Vlad quiet, the voices returned, and I followed their lead. My core began to charge, and my hand sparked. As words began to flow, heat surged beneath my hand increasing to the point of burning. Tendrils of smoke rose from beneath my palm and then the lock clicked to open.

"Hah! You did it!" Vlad said in triumph and pushed the door open.

I checked my hand. The pain had been intense, the sensation of my flesh melting, horribly real and I fully expected the skin on my palm to be singed and blistered, but only a residue of discomfort remained in my fingers and the skin looked completely normal.

Igniting my witch light, I followed Vlad into the funeral home. The first rooms were offices and storage areas, and it wasn't until we made our way to the back of the building that we found a door signed 'Mortuary'.

The clinically white room held an odour of strong disinfectant. Along one wall were cupboards with a countertop overhung with wall units. Immediately in front of this almost kitchen-style set-up were two 'beds' of moulded plastic, each on a pedestal. My knowledge of mortuaries was limited to what I had seen on television where in some hospital scenes there were rows of bodies, each covered with a white sheet. To my immense relief, these 'beds' were empty but on a far wall was a bank of stainless-steel square doors. These had to be the chillers where the bodies were kept.

Thankfully, the chillers were labelled and only two appeared to be occupied. 'Florence Rowbottom', a name I recognised as an elderly lady who had recently passed after a short illness, was written on one. The other read, 'Miranda Cuthbertson'.

"This is her."

My hand hovered close to the door but it was Vlad who pulled at the handle and slid the drawer open. Cold air wafted from the chiller and I took a step back.

"Do not worry, Livitha. She will not bite. At least, not yet!" He chuckled at this joke. "Ah, Mindy," he said pulling back the sheet to reveal her face. He gazed down on the woman. "So beautiful," he sighed.

I was surprised at how peaceful she looked. "How long ... before she wakes?"

"Before sunrise," he said stroking Mindy's cheek. He flinched then frowned and recovered her face.

"What is it?"

"Something is not right. She is dead."

"Yes, she is," I agreed.

"She will not rise ..."

"But she was bitten?"

"Not by a vampire!"

"But her blood was drained!"

"Yes, but not by a vampire."

"Then how did she die?"

He stood silent for a moment, then said, "We will let Mindy tell us."

This confused me to the point where my thoughts became jumbled. "But ... she is dead ... and you said she wasn't going to rise because she wasn't bitten by a vampire. How can she speak?" Another wave of dread washed over me. "Do you mean you want to contact her—on the other side? Because necromancy ... there's no way ..."

"No, not that."

"Then how?"

"In the best crime dramas, the bodies speak the truth." He gestured to Mindy and took a corner of the sheet that covered her. "We must inspect the body."

Vlad pulled back the cover to reveal Mindy's face and neck then bent down close to inspect the wounds. "Livitha, these marks have not been caused by a vampire. The wounds are without bruising. If she were alive when her neck was punctured, there would be bruising. True bruising cannot occur after death. Darker areas appear beneath the skin after death, but this is due to gravity – they call it *livor mortis* – but it is not bruising. This means that the puncture wounds were made after she was dead. No vampire would drain a body of blood after death. It is fatal to us."

"So, what killed her?"

He brushed hair away from her face. "I think it was this." A large bruise bloomed at her hairline and blood was crusted in her hair. "Blunt force trauma that caused a massive haemorrhage in her brain."

I noticed a mark below her sternum. "What's that?" I pulled the cover to reveal a long incision.

Vlad groaned. "Desecrated!" he hissed. "Pass me something."

"Something?"

"Yes, something so I can use to look inside."

"The ... her body?"

"Yes."

My head began to swim, but I followed instruction, checked through the drawers and passed him a likely instrument.

Several minutes passed until he stood back and declared, "She is empty!"

"Empty? What on earth do you mean?"

"Her organs have been removed. Her heart, her liver, her kidneys, they have all gone."

"Gone?"

"Yes! My poor Mindy was bludgeoned to death and then someone drained her of blood and removed her organs."

"This is horrific! There must be a madman in the village."

"That is possible, although there is another consideration; human organs and blood are commodities in today's world," Vlad explained.

"You think that someone is selling her organs?"

"It's possible. They were removed with precision."

I was out of my depth. "We have to call the police!"

Chapter Twenty-Eight

Garrett answered on the third ring and he didn't hold back on his frustration. "Liv! Where are you? You were supposed to come to the station this evening and give your statement. I waited for you."

"Sorry!" I said with a touch of guilt. "But we ... I had to check on something."

"What exactly did you have to check?" There was a note of impatience in his voice.

"I know that Vlad didn't kill Mindy."

"Liv, we can talk about this at the station. Come in tomorrow morning. I'll be waiting. Ten o'clock, okay?"

"No. Garrett, listen. Vlad is innocent."

"Really? And just how did you come to that conclusion?"

"I can prove it. That's what I had to check."

He groaned. "Liv! What exactly have you checked?"

"Mindy was eviscerated."

My statement was met with silence.

"Vlad would never do that!" I continued.

"Liv! Where are you?"

"And Mindy was killed and *then* drained of blood. Vlad only drinks from the living. Vampires don't drink the blood of the dead; it's fatal to them. That's why Vlad is a vegan."

"Vlad is a vegan?"

"Yes, animal flesh makes him sick, or at least gives him the runs!"

"Well ... I guess that's a good reason to go vegan, but, Liv, how do you know that Mindy was eviscerated? That knowledge hasn't been made public."

I glanced at the cadaver realising quite how horrific my explanation would be.

"Liv ...Where are you?"

There was nothing for it; I had to tell the truth. "I'm ... I'm at the morgue."

"What on earth are you doing at the morgue?"

"Well ... Vlad wanted to prove it wasn't him and when she didn't rise, we ... checked the body."

"You checked the body! So, you're *inside* the morgue?"

"Yes! We had to know for sure."

"I cannot believe this! And you examined the body?"

"We had to!"

"Unbelievable!"

"It was the only way!"

"You're breaking the law!"

"I'm sorry ..."

"Is Vlad with you?"

"Erm ... yes."

"Don't do anything to confront him or upset him. I'm on my way, Liv. Leave the building. Don't touch anything. Wait in your car."

I realised that Garrett wasn't convinced of Vlad's innocence. To him I was in the company of a crazed killer. 'Call Ended' appeared on the mobile's screen.

"Is something wrong, Livitha?"

"Yes, I don't think he believes that you're innocent."

"Pah!"

"Vlad, go back to Haligern. You'll be safe there."

"I can't leave you here to face him alone."

"I'm not going to face him. I'm sure he would take me in for questioning and I have to discover who this madman is."

Chapter Twenty-Nine

By the time we left the building the sun was beginning to rise, and I was forced to drive back to Haligern with Vlad in the boot. Covered in blankets like some notorious criminal arriving for a court hearing, I bundled him into the house and down into his cellar-bedroom. After making a cup of tea, and relating the night's events to my aunts, I joined him in the sun-free room.

He sat slumped in his ornately carved chair, hands cupping the dragon's heads that scowled from the end of its arms.

"You know what Dracul means, Livitha?" he said as I took my final step down the stairs.

"No, actually I don't."

"It means dragon." He sighed. "Once I was the most feared man in all the land, now I hide from nagging women and men mock me by killing the women I love!"

I was unsure how to respond. "I'm sure people are still terrified of you, Vlad."

"Hah! No. Now they dress up to mock me. I am a joke."

"Of course you're not a joke," I placated. "You have a huge fan base!" I said trying to appeal to his arrogance. "Just look at Whitby. They have a whole weekend dedicated to you."

"They do?"

"Yes, and it draws people from all over the country."

His lips curled to a faint smile. "Perhaps it is true. My Whitby brides were very enthusiastic when I told them who I was."

"See!" His brides were evidence of his broken promises to my aunts and mention of them made me bristle, but now was not the time for a confrontation. "They adored you before they even met you, and now all they want is you." I said remembering the determined scratching, knocking, and plaintiff calls at the window.

"I suppose you are right, but still, the men mock me—they killed my Mindy!"

Vlad was turning the situation around to be about him, and I had to bite my tongue. Instead, I said, "We should go over all the evidence that we have and try to figure out some leads."

"Leads? Do you mean suspects?"

"Yes. On the way back in the car I started to think over the events of the past few days and there are a number of scenarios I think we should explore."

"Tell me."

"Well, for a start-"

A sharp knock at the cellar door stopped my flow of words.

Vlad shouted an imperious 'Come!' and Aunt Thomasin made rapid steps halfway down the stairs.

"Livitha, you have to come upstairs now. There are police all over the garden. They came in a black van and have guns!"

"A SWAT team?"

"We think so!"

"I'll be up in a moment."

Aunt Thomasin became stern. "Vlad, you must stay down here. They won't find you if you stay in this room."

He nodded. "I will trust the women of Haligern coven with my life."

Back upstairs in the kitchen the energy crackled. An unmarked black van was parked in the driveway along with armed police officers.

"He didn't believe me!" I said with dismay as another car that I quickly recognised as Garrett's, arrived through the gates.

"What are we going to do? We have a fugitive from the law in the cellar."

"Garrett knows that I was with Vlad last night at the morgue. They'll want to take me in for questioning too."

"Pah! Blackwoods! They never change."

"They'll want to arrest Vlad!"

"We simply cannot allow that to happen."

"He would die instantly in the sun."

"I think if the police enter the house and try to arrest him, we may see the worst of Vlad's nature arise," Aunt Loveday said in sombre tones. "Livitha, I will place a protective spell around the house, and particularly over the cellar. You will leave unseen."

"Leave?"

"Yes. We need some time to arrange Vlad's departure."

"But what about the SWAT team? They'll want to come inside."

"I will allow them entrance, but they will discover nothing but a group of elderly women. Now, hurry Livitha, leave by the back entrance whilst I prepare my spell. By the time you walk to your car, they will not be able to see you, but I cannot make that last for long, my energies will be focused on hiding the cellar."

"We can help, Loveday!" Aunt Euphemia said. "If we join our magick together, it will not be such a struggle for you."

My other aunts nodded their agreement.

"Thank you, sisters, but given what happened the last time we attempted to 'pool' our magick I'd rather work alone today."

"Well!" said Aunt Beatrice, "I cannot believe that you still hold that against us after all this time."

Garrett motioned for the team of men to advance on the cottage. "Can you talk about this later," I asked. "They're about to knock on the door!"

"Well, it beggars belief!"

"Ssh! Beatrice," Aunt Euphemia chided. "Go ahead, Loveday. Cast your spell."

Aunt Loveday nodded, told me to make my way to the back of the house and then began her spell weaving. Ancient and powerful, I felt her magick swell even before I had left the room.

I snuck around the back of the house to the corner at the front and scanned the area. Several men in black combat-style uniform stood at the van with their weapons across their chests. Garrett was striding towards the door with even more men following. They were a menacing sight, and I was torn between leaving Haligern to begin my own investigation into Mindy's death and staying to talk to the men so that my aunts didn't have to face their barrage of questions alone. My mind began to imagine the scenario—they would force entrance, breaking the door and riding roughshod over my aunts' protestations. They may even be rough with my aunts! I faltered at the corner as Garrett began to mount the steps.

'Leave!' The voice was faint but there was no mistaking its insistence. *Feran, Befinden cwelland!* 'Leave! Find the killer!"

I took a tentative step away from the corner of the house and then another. The men at the van took no notice of me and although one scanned the side of the house where I stood, he made no indication that he could see me. Still wary, I took slow steps towards my car and then ran the final few feet, then ducking down before opening the door. It was wasted effort on my part. Aunt Loveday's magick was strong and even when I started the engine, and the car began to roll forward, the men didn't notice. Garrett and the team of armed officers entered the house as I left through the gates.

My hands trembled as I shifted the gear into third and accelerated away from the cottage. Mind whirring, I could only think of the men haranguing my aunts, demanding to search the house for evidence of Vlad. They were alone and vulnerable. A sudden thought struck; was it my aunts who were alone and vulnerable or Garrett and his armed team? My aunts were powerful witches and not averse to casting spells simply for their own amusement. My attitude began to change. My aunts may appear to be elderly, but they were also strong women with centuries of experience of dealing with adverse situations. As I considered this, and imagined my aunts conjuring spells to deceive the men, or even transmogrify them - they could become toads or even slugs for a while - my confidence in them grew and my worry diminished. They could take care of themselves. Afterall, I was the pupil, they the teachers.

I drove until I found a turn-off that led to a track into our woodlands then parked the car. I had to gather my thoughts so switched off the engine, confident that I was hidden from the road.

Chapter Thirty

The only thing I knew for certain was that Vlad was innocent; he had tender feelings for Mindy and no motive for murder. Sure, he loved her and wanted her to join him walking in the shadows, but that love ruled him out as her killer.

I had to form my jumbled thoughts into a coherent list so took my notepad and pen and began to write a list of suspects. I wrote Vlad's name at the top of the list but crossed it through. The second name on my list was Martha.

The woman was another suspect, but if killing Mindy had been an act of revenge then she would have passed on the vampire virus and stolen her from Vlad as he had first suspected. That would cause him real pain. I crossed her name from the list.

The Whitby wives were also suspects, but Vlad had hinted at their immaturity, evidenced by their transformation of a cute Pomeranian into a hellish vampire dog with glowing red eyes and a lust for blood. If the wives had killed Mindy, then I felt certain they would not have removed her internal organs with surgical precision. I placed a line through 'Whitby Wives'.

Igor also made the list. He obviously held a grudge towards Vlad and had even been moonlighting for Martha. However, I was unsure of him. Did he have the knowledge to remove the woman's organs in such expert fashion? I doubted it, but I was ignorant of his history, so he remained on the list.

After thinking things through, Igor was the only suspect I had. It was a pathetic effort. I scanned the list:

- ~~Vlad~~
- ~~Martha~~
- ~~Whitby Wives~~
- ~~Igor – revenge killing – Vlad won Igor's fiancé in a game of cards. Igor believes Vlad cheated.~~

I had to be missing something. Closing my eyes, I reimagined the events from the last few days. There had to be other clues!

The first image that popped into my mind was the car that had passed me at speed on the night of the murder. It came from the direction of the morgue, clipping my wing mirror. Whoever was in the car was in a hurry—speeding through fog was dangerous and I was lucky to have escaped with just a clipped wing mirror. I added the unknown person to my list.

- Car driver – white paintwork – speeding through fog from direction of morgue

And then there was what Vlad had said about Mindy's phone call. She had wanted to see him, but the way he had worded her request was odd. At first, I had put it down to a language issue, after all, English wasn't Vlad's first language, but now I wasn't so sure. I closed my eyes again and recalled our conversation. 'Mindy wants to see me. It is urgent. She has

something she must tell me. I must meet her at the morgue.'
Now, the words were loaded with meaning. What had been so
urgent? What was so important that he had to travel at that
time to go and see her? And why did he have to go to the
morgue to speak to her? It was an odd place to arrange a re-
union, even if she did work there. And then I remembered
a previous comment Vlad had made when he'd first told me
about Mindy. She was looking for a new job and hinted about
problems with colleagues. I added the unknown colleague to
my list.

- Problem colleague? Enjoys job, but Mindy looking
  for somewhere else to work.

It was an outlier, but I was willing to consider anything.

As I scanned the list a thought struck me and simultane-
ously made me want to kick myself. I had been so blind! There
was another name to add to the list; the Reverend Parsivall. He
had shown a different side to his character when he had spoken to Mindy at the opening. I recalled the scene. Towering
above her slight figure, he had leaned in, grabbed her elbow,
and hissed 'It's only over when I say it is'. Mindy had tugged at
his grip and told him to get his hands off her to which he had
replied, 'Make me!' There was a history between the two. Were
they having an affair that Parsivall couldn't accept was over? I
added him to my list. It looked a little healthier:

- ~~Vlad~~
- ~~Martha~~
- ~~Whitby Wives~~

- ~~Igor - count won Igor's fiancé in a game of cards. Igor believes Vlad cheated.~~
- Car driver – white paintwork – speeding through fog from direction of morgue
- Problem colleague – enjoys job, but Mindy looking for another morgue to work in.
- Parsivall – threatening to Mindy during the opening. Ex-lover unable to let go?

I mulled over the list and then made a decision. I had no idea which colleague Mindy had issues with and would have to find a contact with knowledge of the morgue's personnel to further that line of enquiry. I could talk to Igor later, once I returned to the cottage. Parsivall had gone to the top of my list, but I had no idea where he lived and would have to ask Dr. Cotta for his address. Mindy herself was my best hope. As I knew where she lived, I decided to search her house for clues about her colleague at the morgue and her relationship with the Reverend Parsivall.

Chapter Thirty-One

Mindy Lived on the Heskitt estate, a large area of land that had belonged to the family since the Black Death when their wily ancestor had taken advantage of the situation and invested heavily in local land. Now the huge country house and farmland were run by the business-savvy Lady Annabelle Heskitt. Mindy's house was a tiny end of terrace cottage that had been built in the late eighteenth-century to house the Heskitt's farm labourers. Parking for the resident's cars was a small carpark at one end of the terrace. It was empty and the only other car was parked outside one of the mid-terrace houses.

I pulled up at the side of the row of terraces and parked the car beneath an overhanging oak. A deeply rutted track wound past the house and up into the hills. The car wasn't exactly camouflaged but at least it wasn't obvious. In such a tiny community, an unfamiliar car would immediately arouse suspicion and what I was about to do was definitely illegal. However, I was on a mission to discover Mindy's killer so felt justified in breaking and entering her house and searching through her belongings. Impressed by my courage, I locked my car and entered the property through a side gate set into a low stone wall. I decided to try the back door first. Although I had successfully unlocked the door at the morgue, I was keen to avoid using my magick; not only did it sap my energy – which, after lack of sleep and the stress of the past few days, was already running low – but it was painful! My hands fizzed and crackled like particularly bad pins and needles. I tried the door. It was locked but I had expected that. Next, I searched for the key, checking under plant pots and the doormat. As I ran my finger over the timbers of the small storm porch that protected the back door, I found it.

"Yes!" I whispered in triumph, surprised that people really did leave door keys hidden. I felt sure it was an omen of success and entered the house.

The back door led straight into the kitchen which was a small space crammed with cupboards of pine with a soft, aged, hue. The floor was laid with red clay tiles and at the centre of the room was small pine table and two chairs. A Belfast sink sat beneath the window and the windowsill was filled with an array of houseplants. A healthy-looking spider plant hung from the ceiling above the drainer. The small patches of wall that could be seen were painted white. It was a pleasant room with a happy energy.

Unsure of quite what I was looking for I made my way to the living room. Again, it was a small room with a single window. The front door was blocked by modern furniture that had been designed for larger rooms and larger people than the house had been built to accommodate. Two sofas covered in mis-matched throws flanked a low coffee table. A cast iron fire, with hearth swept clean, dominated one end of the room. To one side of the chimney breast was a built-in cupboard and shelves. These were stacked with books, photographs, and more houseplants. The photographs appeared to be of a family, but I didn't recognise any of the people in the images. Opening the cupboard revealed a collection of board games and a stack of magazines. There was nothing that I could identify as a clue.

I made my way upstairs. Here there were three rooms; a tiny bathroom, Mindy's bedroom, and a small guest bedroom that doubled as a study. I searched Mindy's room first.

Here, I was surprised by the difference between the upstairs and downstairs rooms. Mindy's bedroom was dominated by a large bed. It was beautifully made with fresh white cotton sheets and plump pillows. A fur throw had been neatly folded at one end. Above the dressing table a large television had been hung on the wall. It gleamed with newness as though just un-boxed. The dressing table was filled with an array of expensive perfumes some still boxed, some with their cellophane wrappers intact. The drawers of her dressing table revealed more expensive items. One drawer was filled with make-up, much of it new and by brands I recognised as from the more expensive brands. Another drawer held jewellery alongside brand new leather gloves of the softest leather. I retrieved an oblong box. 'Cartier' was stamped onto its surface in that brand's distinctive font. Opening it revealed a stunning diamond and emerald bracelet. Again, the box was immaculate.

A check of her wardrobe revealed a similar pattern; there were luxury and designer goods – shoes, coats, dresses, and bags - all in immaculate condition. I took a small black bag sat on a shelf within the wardrobe and examined it. The leather was stamped with the distinctive Gucci logo. I knew that Gucci was an expensive brand so decided to check online to discover its price. A quick search returned results that made my jaw drop. The bag was from their newest range and cost more than two thousand pounds. Where did an assistant at a small-town morgue get the money from to purchase such an expensive bag? My mind returned to Parsivall. Were they gifts? But he was a Reverend, a man of the cloth, and, as far as I knew, the Church of England paid almost a pittance to their priests. He could have his own money of course and, given his accent and self-assurance, that was a possibility. Either that or his funeral business was exceptionally successful!

Next, I checked the guest room.

A small bed was pushed up into a corner of the room, but it also contained a wardrobe and a desk beneath the window. On the desk was a top-of-the-range laptop. Again, it looked new. In the wardrobe was more evidence of newly purchased designer clothes, bags, and shoes. If they weren't gifts, then Mindy had gone on a shopping spree in recent months. If they weren't gifts, then Mindy must have come into a lot of money. It struck me then that she could be a shopaholic—one of those people who purchases things for the buzz. Perhaps that would explain why so many of the items were unopened? I began to wonder if she had money troubles. Did she owe someone a lot of money? Is that why she had been killed? My mind was whirring with different scenarios and populated by more and more sinister underworld characters. I opened the desk's top drawer. It was a disappointment and only contained stationery items. However, in the second drawer was a notepad on which was written a list of names. There were both men and women on the list but two seemed familiar; Francis Barnstaple, an elderly villager who had recently passed away, and Callum Wright, a tragic young man who had been paralysed in a terrible car accident several years ago. As far as I knew, he had died in a hospice. I copied the names and stuffed the paper into my pocket. As I closed the final drawer, which was empty, I noted a piece of paper sticking out from the closed top of her laptop.

Opening the laptop revealed a post-it note. On one note was written 'Keith Cleghorn. 14 BN17 5SJ' along with what appeared to be his telephone number and a date—the same day as the shop's opening! I added this information to the bottom of my list of names then left the house, locking the door behind me.

My next visit had to be to Keith Cleghorn, irritating, weasel-faced journalist from the Liarton Caller.

Chapter Thirty-Two

B ack in the car, I scanned the list of names and the information copied from the post-it notes. Despite my efforts,
there were still only two names that I recognised, but from the
post-it notes I deduced that Mindy had had a meeting with
Keith Cleghorn on the day of the opening and that '14 LN17
5SJ' was in fact the number of his house and postcode. From
the postcode I knew that the man lived in the nearby town but
not the street. That information, I could find the online. With
renewed respect for the usefulness of my mobile phone, I
found the Royal Mail's address finder and punched in the postcode. Within seconds it returned 'Belmont Lane' and I had
Keith Cleghorn's address.

Fuelled by my success, I headed for Belmont Lane with enthusiasm and the certainty that becoming a private investigator
was definitely something I wanted to pursue.

Keith Cleghorn's house was about half a mile beyond the
town's boundary on an older road that gave access to the ancient Wold villages that populated this part of the country.
Fields and a farm sat between Keith's house and the town and
whilst it faced open farmland, it was surrounded by woodland.
I glimpsed the house through the trees and had to reverse to
find the entrance. A gap led to a rough track that ran beside the
house. The track branched to the left about twenty feet from

the road and led to an ungated clearing and Keith's house. It was surprisingly large given its position among the trees and isolation from the town. A lawn with prettily planted borders graced the front of the house whilst a gravelled driveway led to a garage at its side and created a walkway to the front door. The house was of a single storey construction and was double front-ed with clusters of leaves carved into their elaborate wood-en frames. Pierced bargeboard sat beneath a steeply pitched red tile roof. The house was exceptionally pretty and reminded me of the tied cottages on the Blackwood estate although this house was being well maintained and showed no signs of decay. I pulled into the driveway and parked beside a small black car that I presumed was Keith's.

Glad to have found him home, I knocked on the front door with every intention of questioning Keith about his meeting with the now deceased Mindy from the Morgue. After waiting several moments without an answer, I walked to the side of the house. Again, my knock went unanswered and, after checking the back of the house in case he was in his garden, I returned to the side door and tried the handle. It was unlocked and I inched it open, listening out for evidence of movement inside.

"Mr. Cleghorn!"

The door opened into a surprisingly modern, and obvious-ly newly installed, kitchen of glossy white cabinets and black faux-marble counter tops. The space was immaculately clean, and the only evidence of human habitation was a breadboard with two slices of bread waiting to be buttered.

"Mr. Cleghorn!"

I waited at the open door but when no answer came, stepped into the kitchen.

"Keith!"

Again, I waited before taking several more tentative steps. A hallway gave access to the front rooms where I discovered that one was a living room whilst the other was Keith's office.

When the journalist didn't respond to yet another call, I took courage and entered his office. A large desk piled with folders and stacks of papers sat before the bay window. At its centre was an open laptop. A pen lay on a pile of papers at the side of the laptop which suggested Keith was in the middle of working.

With no sign of Keith, I scanned the papers on his desk. There were copious handwritten notes. Some related to assignments, others to meetings at work. I checked through the stacked envelope files. Each one was labelled with a local company or name, some of which I recognised. One label stood out, 'Stanley Calderton/Vicky Stymes' and I remembered the gossip about a respected, very wealthy, local businessman whose empire was discovered to have been built on more nefarious activities than his garlic bread factory. Vicky Stymes, if I remembered correctly, not only managed his dubious import and export business but was his mistress too. A newspaper clipping of a column written by Keith about the scandal was attached to the notes.

I moved to the second pile and my heart skipped a beat. The first file was headed 'Haligern Cottage'. Inside were notes on each of my aunts and clippings from newspapers, some yellowed with age, of unusual stories from the area. There were also photographs including one from the early twentieth century of four elderly women in Victorian dress. The women were my aunts, and the newspaper was dated 1903. Clippings had been collected about the sinkhole incident and to these were attached several sheets of paper with notes as well as photographs from his visit to the shop before it opened. Worse though were photographs from the shop's opening.

Cleghorn had caught the fracas between Vlad and Reverend Parsivall on camera. Of course, Vlad was missing from the image, but Keith had taken a pen and drawn an outline where his figure should have been. There was also a report from another newspaper about three missing women last seen on a hen night in Whitby. I knew instantly that they must be referring to Vlad's Whitby Wives! Keith Cleghorn was collecting evidence against the Coven and Vlad! There was no way I could leave the information, so I took the folder and stuffed it into my bag then continued to search through the files. Another one piqued my interest. 'Dove's Rest Hospice/The Woodlands Crematorium'.

The hospice was where the Reverend Parsivall often sat with the dying, and The Woodlands was the funeral home/mortuary/crematorium where Mindy had worked. I leafed through the papers inside with interest. The first papers were copies of death certificates and I quickly realised that the names matched the ones on the list I had copied at Mindy's house. There were also photographs of Reverend Parsivall that showed him talking to Mindy outside the funeral home. It was obvious he was angry and she fearful, but it was the copy of a newspaper report into the illegal trafficking of human organs that really caught my attention. The piece was several months old but detailed the case of a missing woman who had been found eviscerated. An autopsy revealed that her organs had been removed with surgical precision and linked the case to one several months prior, in the same area of the country.

As I pawed over the information, I heard a groan. Instantly frozen, I listened.

The groan repeated.

It was muffled but appeared to be coming from the sofa. It was then I noticed the blood. Spattered on the carpet, and close to the sofa, patches glistened.

The groan repeated.

Hair rising on my neck, I removed the cushions and fold-out bed. Inside, stuffed into the space beneath, and curled in the foetal position with his hands and feet bound, his mouth taped, was Keith Cleghorn.

All thoughts of the investigation gone, I reassured him that he was safe and dialled 999. The call connected and I gave details of the emergency along with the address then began to untie Keith's hands and feet but as I removed the tape, he gave a final groan and his breathing stopped.

With his blood still wet on my fingers, I backed away from the body. Wheels crunched over the gravel in the driveway and I turned with relief to the window, but the vehicle that pulled up in front of the house wasn't the ambulance I was expecting. The same car that had sped past me from the direction of the morgue on the night Mindy was killed, a white Lexus with a broken wing mirror, pulled into the driveway. My stomach flipped as the Reverend Parsivall stepped out, and I jumped into the shadows as he scanned the house with narrowed eyes. After first stopping to inspect my car, he disappeared down the side of the house.

For a moment I panicked.

I had to hide.

As I scanned the room for refuge, footsteps clacked across the kitchen floor. Sweat began to bead at my brow. There was nowhere to hide!

The voices in my head began to jumble with my panicked thoughts. Aunt Loveday had made me invisible to the police as they had arrived at the cottage, I had to become invisible again. As Parsivall entered the hallway I had only seconds to act. I grabbed the file about Parsivall and the crematorium and darted behind the door just as he stepped into the office. Even a whisper would betray me as, fingers tingling, I delved into the depth of my knowledge, calling on my ancestors for help, then began the silent recitation of ancient words. Parsivall stepped further into the room, becoming still as he noticed the open sofa. I recited the charm with increased effort, mouthing silent words. He swivelled, and just as our eyes met, a shimmering, iridescent film parted us A frown of confusion slid onto his face, but he did a full circle, then stepped towards the body.

Confident that I couldn't be seen, I left the house and jumped into my car, terrified that at any moment Parsivall would descend upon me.

Chapter Thirty-Three

With every passing second behind the wheel, I expected the Reverend to jump out of the house and lumber after me with a pickaxe in hand. Maniacal eyes would stare at me through the window and he would smash at the glass. Painful, rapid beats hammered in my chest as I shoved the key at the ignition with trembling hands. Gripping the steering wheel, I locked my eyes to the house, flitting between the side door and the front door in case Parsivall should throw the door open and begin his attack. The key missed and slipped from my hand. I was certain that as I raised my head from retrieving them in the footwell he would be staring at me with hate-filled, murderous eyes, but the doors remained closed. I retrieved the key, started the engine, and reversed whilst coaching myself to remain calm then focused on driving away from the house. Only when the speedometer read 70mph did I check the rear-view mirror for the white car with the broken wing mirror. The road was clear, and I heaved a sigh of relief whilst maintaining my speed.

I heard the sirens first and automatically slowed at the sound. On the opposite side of the road blue lights flashed and an ambulance hurtled towards me then sped past. Two police cars, lights flashing, sirens blaring, followed close behind. They had to be responding to my 999 call and, if Parsivall was still at the house, then he would get a horrible surprise and hopefully be arrested for the cruel murder of Keith Cleghorn.

As the road straightened, I accelerated to 80mph then slowed as the road dipped. Ahead was a small area of woodland. A favourite spot with dog walkers, it had a small parking area where I could pull in, gather my thoughts, and check through the evidence I had taken from Keith's office. The image of Keith curled up in the sofa bed's base was burned into my mind and I pulled into the parking area with relief. Trembling hands turned off the ignition and, as the engine cut, I sagged against the steering wheel unable to hold back the sob of despair I felt at Keith's passing. I didn't know Keith other than as an annoying weasel-faced journalist who bothered us about the sinkhole incident but grieved for the pain and suffering he must have endured. That he had passed on terrified, horrified me. Dr. Cotta had the Reverend completely wrong. He wasn't a 'friend at the end' nor was he the 'good guy'. In fact, he was quite the opposite—a sociopathic monster. It was a fake persona he hid behind, a fake persona no one would suspect could be so cruel. I pulled the file from my bag and began to read the clippings and photocopied papers carefully.

Memories of the night I had dinner with Dr. Cotta repeated. The Reverend Parsivall had asked him to sign a death certificate and Dr. Cotta had done so without the blink of an eye as though it were common practice for doctors to sign death certificates presented by members of the clergy in a fantasy themed restaurant as they served dinner. Was Dr. Cotta involved too? It would make sense if he were. Who better to be friends with, to flatter and buy gifts for, than a doctor who would sign the death certificates quickly so that the bodies could be 'processed' rapidly and then their organs removed for quick redistribution to the next person in the chain?

As I removed the last sheaf of paper, I noticed writing half-way down the back of the folder. Holding it to the light, I took a closer look. The writing appeared to be the address of a web-site along with what could be a username and password. I keyed the website address into my mobile's browser. It returned the homepage of a cloud storage website. I tapped 'Cleghorn 1969' into the username field and then the final piece of information, a random mix of letters, numbers, and symbols, into the pass-word box. The screen faded then returned a page with a selec-tion of files. I was in!

There were three items in the storage space. The first was a partially written piece by Keith about the trafficking of human organs. The second contained scanned copies of the death cer-tificates, whilst the third was a voice recording. I clicked play and listened to Keith interview Mindy from the Morgue. Ini-tially, Mindy was reluctant to talk, but Keith had obviously been doing his own detective work and set out exactly what he knew of activities at the morgue and her involvement. He could help her if she would only share her troubles. At first Mindy told a story of how she had discovered that the organs of the deceased were being removed illegally and suspected that her boss, and the Reverend Parsivall, were involved. Something in her voice told a different truth and Keith obviously shared the same concerns, teasing information from the woman with surprising skill for a backwater reporter.

As the interview progressed, Mindy admitted that she had known about the operation for some time but was growing in-creasingly uneasy about the whole situation and was now unable to sleep well, the guilt being too much. By the time the interview had ended I had a completely different opinion of the woman. Mindy had been involved with the organ harvesting and trafficking operation from the beginning, and even boasted at what a good team she and her then boyfriend, the Reverend Parsivall made. In a previous job, Parsivall had been a butcher and worked quickly and efficiently. The lucrative operation ran smoothly, being almost 100% profit and, in harvesting from the dead, no one was being harmed. However, the Reverend had grown greedy, wanting ever more bodies, and had put increasing pressure on her by suggesting they move beyond the morgue to satisfy the insatiable needs of their international buyers. When she had read about a murdered woman, killed then eviscerated in a town only thirty miles away, she knew that Parsivall was responsible. This had been the final straw and she had ended their relationship and refused to participate in the crimes any longer. However, Parsivall had become threatening. As the interview closed, two things were obvious: Mindy was terrified of Parsivall and deeply regretted the oversharing of information about her involvement.

I now understood why she had been so keen to befriend Vlad; she was grooming him as her protector.

I closed the webpage and sat back in my seat. This was a crime of the most heinous kind and the killer was still on the loose. I was out of my depth. Calling the authorities was my only option whatever the consequences. I dialled Garrett's number, but as the phone rang a shadow fell across the screen. On the other side of the door a figure blocked the light and, as the phone went to voicemail, I turned to the cold green eyes of Reverend Parsivall.

Chapter Thirty-Four

As Parsivall's eyes bored into mine, I threw the phone down and started the engine. With the door already locked, thanks to the automatic central locking system, Parsivall hammered at the window. I held my nerve, shifted the gear into reverse, did a rapid, perfectly executed three-point turn, and left the car park with squealing tyres.

However, Parsivall was quick to react and was soon tailing close behind. As I accelerated, so did he, and within the next minutes his more powerful car drew up beside mine and we drove in parallel for several moments. With my focus on the road ahead, I accelerated but there was no way I could outrun him.

In the next moment, he slammed his car into mine. The phone flew from the seat and landed in the footwell. Forced to the verge, I tried to steer the car back to the road, but another side swipe shoved me closer to the hedgerow. Branches screeched as they scratched along the bodywork. Ahead, a tree loomed. With the larger, heavier car hugging my side and trapping me in position, I had no option but to slow down and stopped just feet away from its thick trunk. Parsivall slowed with me and then immediately reversed. Blocked by the tree, I had to reverse but, before I had a chance to change gear, I was shunted forward with such force that the car hit the tree and my world became black.

I woke to darkness, intense cold, and clinking metal.

My hands were bound together and, as I moved, I realised I was in the narrow confines of a box. Breathing was difficult and my nose, blocked in one nostril, felt stuffy. The metallic taste of blood filled my taped mouth. My head throbbed. I remained still, listening to the clink of metal then discerned footsteps and whistling. The clink of metal reminded me of hospital scenes from television dramas where the surgeon drops a used instrument into a metal kidney-shaped dish. I imagined Parsivall bearing down on me, a bright light strapped to his forehead, his hands gloved, his face masked, and huge, razor sharp scalpels held aloft ready to ... a sensation of floating overwhelmed me and for several moments I receded into a dark state of unconsciousness. 'Livitha Erikson!' The voice came from somewhere tucked deep at the back of my head. Brilliant light glowed behind my closed eyes. 'Livitha Erikson, daughter of Soren! Rise. Fight for your life.'

With the voices swimming, unsure of reality, I opened my eyes. The box was dark, but there were chinks of light. I focused on my bound hands and light began to glow as a small witch light grew. This time, I kept it small, and cupped it between my bound hands. It gave just enough light to illuminate my stomach area. The box was of smooth pine, and the chinks of light came through small gaps where the strips of timber were separating. I shone the light around and realised I was in what appeared to be a narrow wardrobe laid on its back. Above me was the door. Relief didn't quite flood me, but I did feel reassured. I wasn't encased in a coffin with an unbreakable lock, I was in a wooden wardrobe with numerous areas of weakness. I was also relatively uninjured and able to think clearly. Despite being Parsivall's captive I was confident I had the upper hand. Parsivall was a mortal, an evil killer, yes, but without any power other than brute force. I, on the other hand, was a witch and I was determined to use my magick against him. I focused on the plastic cable tie that bound my hands.

The cable ties transformed. Instead of hard plastic they became soft, grew round then began to wriggle apart, falling off my wrists like worms dropping from a fork of newly dug earth.

With my hands free, I listened. The clinking had stopped along with the noise of Parsivall moving about. He was still whistling but the noise came from the distance. This was my chance. I pushed at the wardrobe door. It gave a little but was obviously locked and there wasn't enough room for me to pull my knees up and kick at the door and if I began to bang on the wood it would alert Parsivall. I pushed at the sides. The wood had the dryness of age which confirmed my first thoughts; it was old and its joints weakening. I manoeuvred myself onto my side and, with my back pushed up against the wardrobe and my knees pulled up to my chest, pushed with my feet. The wood creaked and gave a little. I listened for Parsivall and, sure that he was still out of the room, put pressure on the side of the wardrobe. Joints creaked, wooden seams parted, and light filtered through widening gaps. I waited again, listening to the far-off whistling, and decided to go for it. With massive effort I pushed at the side of the wardrobe. Wood creaked and the joints began to split and then the wardrobe collapsed. Releasing myself from the wooden prison, I found myself in a workshop.

Whitewashed brick walls were lined with racks of neatly stored tools. A long bench filled one wall. A vice was clamped at one end. A large circular saw sat at its middle. The workshop smelled of sawn wood and oil. With double doors at one end and an inspection pit in the middle of the floor, it had been built as a garage. Night had fallen and stark light filled the room. The double doors were ajar and there was no sign of Parsivall.

Chapter Thirty-Five

With my head pounding, unsure if my nose was broken or just bleeding, I stumbled to the garage doors. Lights shone from a downstairs room in a house I could barely discern but, from the rustling of leaves and the lack of noise from car engines, I had to be somewhere deeply rural, somewhere no one would hear me shout!

I decided to head for the dark woodlands that surrounded the property where, once hidden, I could gather my thoughts. Clouds shifted from the moon and light illuminated the area enough to see a large oak in the middle of a lawn. Beyond that a bank of trees marked the edge of the woodlands. I headed for the oak, crunching over pebbles, and threw myself to the dark side. Catching my breath, I set off at a sprint for the safety of the woodland but was immediately yanked back as Parsivall grabbed my collar. Pain spread through my skull as my head crashed against the tree. Taken by surprise, unable to use my magick, I was forced to the ground where Parsivall bound my wrists and tethered me to a tree. With the rope secured to an overhead branch and my arms held aloft, I was trapped!

"You should have kept your nose out of my business, you stupid old bag!" Green eyes scowled at me through narrowed slits.

"You won't get away with this!" I managed. "The police know where I am!"

"Really? Are you sure about that? If that's true, then where are they? Huh? You've been here for a few hours now, so I think it's safe to assume that they don't!" He spat the last words. "Anyway," he said in an offhand way, his demeanour changing as though a switch had been flicked, "we're wasting time. I have orders to fulfil. At least this time I can offer very fresh produce, although the liver may be a little fatty. I'll be back in a moment, just wait there." He snickered then stamped away across the yard and disappeared into the garage. From inside came the clinking of metal. I writhed against my ties, certain that I was going to become his 'very fresh produce', but the rope was too tight, and the past hours had taken their toll; I was low on energy and pain was burning across my back and shoulders. As the clinking continued, panic rose, and any efforts to kick-start my magick failed. It was then that the voices began to speak. I welcomed them with relief as they filled my head. *Livitha, fight*, they repeated. This wasn't helpful. I was trying to fight, but with low energy and magick that was failing to ignite, I was at the mercy of the monstrous Reverend.

Speak to her! Call for help!

Again, not useful.

The voices continued, a singsong of ululating words. *Call her. Ask for help. Mindy. Call Mindy.*

"Mindy? But she's dead!". For the first time, the voices were failing me. "How on earth can a dead woman help me?"

Call Mindy, the voices insisted. *Ask for help.*

"How can I? She's dead!" I shouted in frustration.

Call her!

"Fine! Mindy!" I whispered. "Mindy!"

Of course, nothing came of me whispering the dead woman's name.

Call to the dark realm!
Call to her and she will come!
Necromancer!

"Necromancer!" A chill ran through me. My aunts and I had discussed necromancy, but the unanimous conclusion was that it wasn't a practice we wanted to explore, at least not in a practical sense. Certainly, it had been decided, I needed schooling in the art, but only in a theoretical sense; no one wanted to commune with the dead, at least not through necromancy. Apparently, entering another realm with the permission of the gatekeepers, to speak with past loves and ancestors was something else entirely, quite above board, and acceptable. True necromancy, on the other hand, held the taint of black magick and could have unpredictable, unwanted, consequences. However, my situation was critical and if ancient, ancestral voices were urging me on, I would take their advice and attempt to contact Mindy.

With little hope of it working – I couldn't even get my fingers to spark! – I closed my eyes. During our discussion, Aunt Loveday and then Aunt Thomasin had argued the merits of several schools of thought. There were a number of ways necromancy could be practiced they had explained. With the noise of clinking metal and something being dragged across the garage floor in the background, I began to recall the details of their conversation. As I focused, the voices began to offer ancient words. I had no choice other than to trial a method that invoked a gatekeeper and involved a sacrifice. I had nothing to sacrifice other than to make a promise of service and trembled as I recited the charm. As I recited, my consciousness receded into a dark place within my mind and then opened into another space. I had the distinct, very peculiar sensation of leaving my earthly body although there was no hovering above the scene. Instead, I was transported to another space and as I continued to recite, a figure appeared in my peripheral vision. Despite my efforts, the figure remained indistinct and at the edge of my vision. I sensed its being, and the power it exuded was immense, and horribly dark.

"Livitha, daughter of Haligern Coven, speak your needs."

The voice chilled me but what I needed became clear. "Oh, most powerful, most feared gatekeeper, I am in danger and am desperate for help. I ask for commune with Mindy who passed into your realm yesterday."

"What is your sacrifice?"

"I ..." I stumbled. I had no idea what I could sacrifice. For a moment Lucifer popped into my mind but I instantly dismissed the thought. "I ... I'm not sure."

"Then let me make a suggestion."

I nodded.

"You must honour me by accepting a request in the future."

With my life on the verge of being extinguished, I agreed. "Yes! Yes, that's fine," I said with relief. "Yes, that's fine." The sense of sinking doom washed through every cell in my body. It was an agreement I would live to regret.

"Then call to your messenger. Make your case, but I warn you, she may not listen. Many here are immune to the suffering of the living."

"Thank you!" I said as the figure melted from my peripheral vision. "Mindy," I called. "Mindy! Please talk to me. I need your help!" Moments passed and nothing happened but as I called her name again a light appeared in the distance and grew to push back the darkness. As in all the old-fashioned ghost movies Mindy was a translucent and colourless form of her living self. Thankful that she didn't bear any of the wounds of her death, I faced her. Her eyes were glazed, and she made no effort to speak or respond as I made my petition for help—to go to Vlad and tell him I was in danger.

Without a word, the deathly pale version of Mindy disappeared. I had no idea whether she would take my message to Vlad or not.

Chapter Thirty-Six

I returned to full consciousness, pain wracking my upper body, and the noise of Parsivall working in the garage. The ting of metal was followed by the grinding whirr of power tools and then something was dragged across the floor accompanied by grunts of effort.

Hung like a pheasant waiting to be plucked, I listened to the scraping noises, dreading the moment when they stopped. Light brightened in the garage and then Parsivall opened both garage doors. I began to tremble. At the centre of the room were two tables. One large with a tilted metal surface and two buckets placed to catch whatever drained through the holes cut through its lower end, and another smaller table, sat to the side. Unlike the larger table, this one was laid out with tools. I had no doubt it had been prepared for me. Again, I struggled against my ties. The rope chafed at my skin, but there was no way of releasing them. I made frantic efforts to call on the magick I had used to release the cable ties, but my energy was so low from communing with the dark realm and Mindy, and my mind so scrambled, that I could only manage several flickers of light and a single spark from my fingers.

Was this it? Was this my end?

Parsivall stepped out of the garage and walked with purpose across the yard. "Are you ready, nosey parker?" he called as he walked towards me.

Without magick to protect me, I called on his conscience. "How can you do this? You're a Reverend? You claim to be a man of God! A holy man!" It was a pathetic effort; the man was about as holy as an abandoned dog's turd and he merely snorted without any prick of conscience. I became angry. "You're a hypocrite! A monster!"

Again, there was no indication that my words bit into any compassionate sensibilities he may have once had.

"Sorry, to keep you waiting," he said with a smile that chilled my bones. "But you know what they say ..."

"No!"

"I'll tell you then. Good things come to those who wait." He withdrew a hammer from behind his back.

I mewled and pulled at the ropes.

He took a step towards me, hammer raised, its shiny surface glinting in the moonlight. As his arm began to descend, Parsivall, and the hammer, disappeared as though a magic trick had been performed. Pained grunts followed and then he rose above a mass of black cloth until his feet left the ground. With Vlad's huge hand clamped around his neck, staring eyes bulged as he squirmed. With superhuman strength the ancient vampire lifted the man higher then threw him with enormous force. Parsivall hurtled through the air and smashed against the brick wall of the garage. Vlad disappeared only to reappear beside the man, again picking him up by the throat. This time, with Parsivall bucking against his grip, Vlad walked back to me. Gasping for breath, he spluttered and choked as his wrists were tied and the end of the rope thrown over a sturdy branch. He was hoisted aloft, and the rope secured around the trunk. With Parsivall a captive, Vlad broke my ties and caught me as I fell. Minutes passed as he cradled me in his arms, waiting for my relieved sobbing to stop.

"Thank you!" I managed whilst gripping his sleeve. Being wrapped in his arms felt safe and I dreaded the moment when he would release me.

"Please, do not thank me. I should never have let you go out alone. If I had known what trouble you would find I would not have let you go." He shuddered. "If Mindy had not come ..." He gave me a final, reassuring squeeze, then helped me to my feet.

With Vlad at my side, and Parsivall no longer a danger, calm restored within me and I felt my energies return. My thoughts, no longer scrambled, began to focus. I related exactly what had happened since I'd left Haligern Cottage, explaining the organ harvesting and trafficking operation Parsivall was running, how he groomed the dying and would remove their organs at leisure in the mortuary of the funeral home and sell them on the international, highly illegal, black market. I also explained Mindy's part in the crime and how, as Parsivall had become greedy and taken to killing in order to harvest the organs, she had tried to leave.

"This must have been what she was trying to tell me on the night she was murdered."

"Yes, it could be. It would also explain why Parsivall was threatening her at the opening. He killed Mindy, Vlad, and the journalist she confided in."

"And he was about to kill you." Vlad's attention turned to the man bucking like a worm caught on a fishing hook. A gleam of pure and malicious joy passed over his face. As he stood before Parsivall he rubbed his hands. "Now you will know why they called me Vlad the Impaler."

Parsivall made a mewling noise of terror, grabbed at the rope holding his wrist, then sagged against the tree as he realised there was no hope of escape. I grimaced. Parsivall was a monster, and I had no sympathy for the man, but I couldn't stand by and watch Vlad perform his 'party trick'.

"Would you mind ... terribly ... if I sorted him out, Vlad?"

He cast me an appreciative glance. "It would be my pleasure." With a gracious sweep of his arm accompanied by a small bow he said, "The stage is all yours, Livitha, son of Soren Erikson."

I sighed with exasperation. "Daughter, Vlad! I'm his daughter."

"Of course I know this, it is just my little joke. It brightens my shadows to have a little fun. Now, Livitha, finish him!" His following chuckle had a low and disturbingly sociopathic ring to it. "Electrocute him with your powers! Cook his organs with your magick! Do your thing, as the modern people say."

"Well ..." I drew my arms back as if to throw supercharged currents at Parsivall through my fingers. The man whimpered. "I think I can do something similar."

I began to recite an ancient charm, calling on my ancestors magick, and focused all of my energy on the tree. Its leaves trembled and then the entire tree with its generous canopy of branches shuddered. As I felt the power run through me and cross to the tree, branches began to grow and twist, moving through the air and curling down towards the cowering figure of the Reverend. He squealed as a tendril of wood wound around one leg and then another. In the next moment thick branches wrapped around his torso and others shot forward to weave a prison of wood.

"There!" I said in triumph as green eyes stared in terror from gaps between the leaves and twigs.

Vlad seemed unimpressed.

"Well, I know it's not what you'd do," I said, "but he has to face trial for what he has done."

"Pah! You are too soft."

"True, but two wrongs don't make a right."

"Pah!" Vlad turned from me with a sniff. "I ... well ..." He returned to face me. "I do not approve, but he is your prisoner, and you must do as you see fit."

"Thank you!"

He returned my smile revealing bone-white, inch-long fangs. "Now, your aunts are waiting, and we must not inconvenience those wonderful ladies a moment longer."

I sighed, suddenly weary. "It's a long way home and I've lost my phone. Can you call a taxi?"

"Tsk! Why do we need the vehicles of mortals when we can fly?" With a sweep of his cape Vlad transformed into a bat. He swooped towards me, eyes locking onto mine. Huge black eyes glistened in the moonlight, staring out from the cutest, furriest bat face I had ever seen. "Fly with me!" he squeaked. I repressed my desire to coo at how cute and furry he was and managed to agree before, with a flap of his wings, he shot upwards.

Witch light in hand, I scanned the area around the tree looking for a suitable branch. Finding none, I ran back to the garage where I remembered seeing a broom. Standing against the wall was a sturdy yard brush with a wide bar and thick bristles. It was the best I could do and an improvement on Mrs. Driscoll's plastic affair used during my inaugural flight.

Under moonlight, with a furry vampire bat hovering above me, a serial-killing false priest tied to a tree at my side, and the yard brush between my legs, I recited the ancient words of flight and rose into the night sky for the second time in my life. Just as with the first flight, it was joyous, and I flew back to Haligern, and my aunts, with Vlad at my side and a huge grin plastered to my face, all worries, and trauma forgotten.

Chapter Thirty-Seven

It was the evening on the day after Parsivall had attempted to kill me and, for the third time in as many days Garrett was at Haligern's front door. I was only surprised that he hadn't come sooner.

The doorbell rang and this time I answered. With it being dark outside, I couldn't ask Garrett and his colleague to wait in the garden so showed them into the drawing room.

"Tea?" I asked with a bright smile although my hands trembled. The reality of what had happened hit that morning and, despite having slept well, I woke with a familiar sense of anxiety that I hadn't been able to shift throughout the day.

When I returned to the room, I placed the tray on a side table and poured Garrett and his colleague, PC W. Harker, a cup of tea. Towering above me, hair on her top lip caught the light as I passed the cup and saucer, but it was the three hovering figures at the French doors that made my hands shake. The cup clinked in the saucer and liquid sloshed over the side. "Sorry! I'm still a little shaken," I explained as the tremble in my hand increased.

With a look of concern, Garrett placed a hand on my shoulder. "Sit down, Liv. You've had an ordeal."

I nodded, thankful that his back was to the doors and desperately sought for a way of closing the curtains without drawing his attention. As I failed to think of a way, the women floated out of view and I sat down with relief.

Garrett and his over-sized blonde colleague sat to face me.

"So, Liv, the police are not going to press charges this time, and we've put some of the inconsistencies in your statement down to stress."

"Completely understandable." PC Harker sounded genuine and I felt a little warmer towards her.

"Yes, completely, given the circumstances, but ... well ... I need your assurance that it won't happen again."

"I think I can assure you that I won't be chased through the countryside and be taken captive by a serial killer any time soon," I said in a lame effort to make light of the experience.

Something clinked in the fireplace and then I felt a familiar displacement of air. I took a sip of tea with a trembling hand sure that a fairy had just shot down the chimney. Increasingly on edge, with the fear that Vlad's Whitby Wives would make another surprise appearance and a fairy would start playing its tricks, I was glad that Aunt Euphemia had dropped one of her calming elixirs into my cup before I'd left the kitchen. 'I think you'll need it, darling,' she'd said as I'd tried to dissuade her. She had been right.

"You know what I mean, Liv. Recently, when there's been a murder, the trail has led to your door and I've had quite a lot of trouble at the office."

"There have only been two murders!" I said in my defence. "You make it sound so awful."

"Murder is awful, Liv."

"Yes, of course, I know that, but I couldn't help being involved!"

Garrett raised a brow.

"Okay, yes, I know that I was perhaps more involved with the investigations than I should have been, but ... I just had to discover the truth. And I did!"

"Yes. I know, but that's my job, really, and I know that you were keen to clear your guest's name, but ... well, it got you into trouble - nearly fatal trouble - and my superior wanted to charge you with hindering the progress of a murder investigation!"

"Even though I discovered who really did it?"

"Yes," he said sternly. "We have procedures that have to be followed. You have contaminated several crime scenes. That could muddy the waters of our investigation and make it harder to build a case against the guilty parties. Listen, I don't want to see you on the wrong side of the law and ..." his voice softened, "and I don't want to see you hurt."

Saying 'thank you' seemed inadequate and I bit my lip. He looked so handsome as he sat opposite me and the desire to reach over, close my eyes, and wait for his lips to gently kiss mine, was almost unbearable. I quickly, and very clumsily, diverted the conversation. "So ... Dr. Cotta ... he wasn't involved?"

A flicker of pain, that mirrored my own, passed over Garrett's face, and he became officious. "There's no evidence to suggest that he knew anything about it. So far, our investigations can only conclude that he was being duped by the Reverend. I can't go into details, but as far as we are aware, he wasn't an accomplice, not a willing one anyway."

I sighed with relief and then felt awash with shame. I had immediately jumped to the conclusion that Dr. Cotta was involved. In my mind he had been guilty of atrocities too.

"So, Miss Erikson," Garrett's mannish colleague said. "We've managed to withhold some of the details of yesterday's incident. The newspapers will only report that Parsivall was found tied to a tree, not that he was bound by its branches. Your name has also been withheld and won't appear in any local, or national newspapers."

"Thank you!" Genuinely grateful, I offered a smile in return but as our eyes met, the hovering trio of vampires reappeared at the window. They were gone in a second, but not before PC Harker had followed my distracted gaze.

"Vermin!" she hissed and flew into action, jumping out of her seat and withdrawing a wooden stake from an inner pocket and revealing a belt of tools in the process. I spotted a hunting knife, a wooden cross, and a row of sharpened wooden stakes.

"Vampire hunter!" I said the words aloud before I had a chance to think. "She's a vampire hunter!"

Startled by my outburst and her sudden jump into action, Garrett turned to his colleague. "Not here, Mina!" was his terse reply.

I was about to express my surprise at his lack of surprise and lacklustre command to stand-down when a knock at the door was immediately followed by Vlad walking through it.

I was not prepared for what happened next.

Vlad froze.

PC Harker rose to her full height and grew tense, locked in a fighting stance.

"Mina!" he managed to gasp. "My Mina!"

Mina! Could this well-built and muscular woman really be his Mina?

Mina jumped forward, her arm held aloft, the sharpened stake ready to stab at Vlad. Only Garrett's quick actions saved the Count's life as he launched himself at Mina and grappled her to the floor.

"Mina!" he chided as she lay pinned to the floor. "Give it a rest!"

I was even more surprised when Vlad began to laugh, this time a deep and hearty chuckle. "Oh, my Mina. You will never change."

"Vlad, what is going on?"

"It is my Mina! I have found her."

Garrett warned Mina to behave herself then allowed her to stand.

I stared from Vlad, his eyes glittering with joy, to the Amazonian blonde with bulging thighs and a hairy top lip, her face too masculine to be called pretty, and said, "Are you telling me that the woman you love, the woman whose soul you chase through the shadows, is a vampire hunter?"

"Yes!"

"But she's a vampire hunter, Vlad, and you're a vampire! That means it's her job to kill you!"

"That is true, but society has changed. Perhaps now our love will not be forbidden?"

At his words Mina visibly relaxed. "Do you think so?" she asked and took a step towards Vlad. Garrett flinched, reaching a hand across her waist to halt her progress. She handed him the stake.

"Yes, Mina. Yes, I do." Holding his arms wide, he said, "Come to me, my Mina."

No longer held back by Garrett, Mina threw herself into Vlad's arms.

What followed was a display of affection that began tentatively but then exploded into a full-blown and passionate kiss. I turned away from the amorous pair with growing discomfort and walked to the hearth, poking at the embers and warm ashes from last night's fire hoping they'd soon calm down. Garrett joined me, mumbling something I couldn't quite hear. Embers sparked, glowed, then died out and I caught a miniature face peering out from behind the large clock at the centre of the mantelpiece. I glared at the tiny fairy, hoping it would understand my silent instruction to hide. In the periphery of my vision, three figures pressed up against the French doors. I groaned inwardly, but then realised that given Garrett's reaction to Mina and Vlad, he must have known she was a vampire hunter and was okay with her snogging the face off Count Dracula in my drawing room. If that were the case, then seeing three vampires hovering at my French windows and a fairy flitting about my mantelpiece wouldn't be such an issue. I managed to relax a little. "So," I said. "Mina? Her name badge says PC W. Harker?"

"Yeah, her name is Wilhelmina, but she hates it, so we call her Mina."

"And is she *the* Mina Harker?" I said referring to Bram Stoker's novel.

"Maybe," he answered with a shrug.

"And you knew she was a vampire hunter?"

"It's not something I can talk about, Liv?"

Already piqued, my interest went into overdrive, the smooching pair behind me forgotten. "That's an interesting answer."

"I guess," he said and glanced at the lovers but quickly returned to staring into the fire.

"Is there much call for vampire hunters on the police force?"

"That's also a question I'm not at liberty to answer."

I poked the fire with frustration and was about to question him further when Vlad coughed, signalling the end of his embrace with Mina. Garrett turned to them with obvious relief and I turned with a renewed determination to discover his secrets but threw a genuinely happy, if slightly bemused, smile at Vlad.

"I have found her again!" he beamed, his arm around Mina's waist. Head resting on his shoulder, her cheeks were flushed which made the hairs on her top lip appear a little darker. "No more shall I walk in the shadows now that I have found my Mina."

I wasn't convinced of this; Mina's modus operandi was to turn up and then disappear again, and again. However, determined to help Vlad keep her this time, I made a mental note to talk to my aunts about a spell that could help keep them together.

The noise of scratching at the French doors caught Vlad's attention. "Ah, my brides!" he said without any indication of embarrassment or unease and moved from Mina's side to open the door.

"No, Vlad! Don't you dare invite them in!" I blurted, horrified at the thought of the less than sane women coming inside.

"But I thought people were more accepting of different lifestyles these days?" He looked crestfallen.

"They are," I spluttered, realising I had offended Vlad. "It's just well ..." I scrabbled with my thoughts; I didn't want the women in the house, but they were Vlad's 'family' now. They continued to hover at the door, looking more dishevelled than they had at the opening and obviously not thriving in the village wilds. My resolve not to let them inside the cottage began to crumble, but as Vlad looked at me with a pout and huge, imploring eyes that reminded me of the super-cute bat he had transformed into, and I opened my mouth to concede, Mina stepped between Vlad and the women.

"People may be more accepting these days, Vlad, and there are many faults that I am willing to accept," she said this with a meaningful look, "but I am not going to put up with *them*!" She jabbed a finger at the Whitby Wives who had now been joined by their miniature hellhound. Red eyes stared into the room from the furry white face of the Pomeranian, its diamante collar glinting in the light. Breath steamed over the glass as it yapped. In the next moment Mina launched into action, grabbing the wooden stake from Garrett's hands, and flinging open the French doors.

Flying kung-fu style across the patio, one booted, muscular leg horizontal, she floored the tallest wife. With the woman on the ground, Mina did a forward flip and landed on her torso, pinning her to the ground, the wooden spike raised. "Vlad!" I called as he made no effort to intervene. "She's going to kill them!"

The night filled with inhuman shrieks as, with expertise honed over centuries, Mina tackled the wives and released them from their undead existence.

"Yes!" Vlad replied as he looked on with admiration. "And isn't she magnificent!"

EPILOGUE

Several weeks had passed after Vlad's departure when a package carrying a Transylvanian postmark arrived.

Aunt Loveday had been gone all morning and we waited until after lunch for her return before curiosity got the better of us and we opened the parcel.

Inside was a letter and a painting. It was a painting of the Count and Mina standing before a grand fireplace in the castle's ballroom. A huge and ornate gilded mirror reflected the room and, as this was a painting, it reflected them too. Dressed in a black velvet dress that showed off her trim waist and muscular arms, Mina stood beside the count, blonde hair piled high with a diamond tiara. The pair smiled back at me, obviously happy. An extremely fluffy miniature Pomeranian sat by their feet.

"Oh, that's so sweet!" Aunt Beatrice cooed.

"She didn't run away this time," I said as I admired the pair.

"The letter says that she has taken up interior design and is remodelling the rooms at the castle," Aunt Euphemia reported. "The Count mentions that it's much quieter at home these days."

Aunt Thomasin laughed. "I wonder if she despatched all his brides?"

"Given the way she 'despatched' the Whitby Wives, I wouldn't be surprised!" I said remembering the speed with which she had dealt with the women. It had taken her less than three minutes to relieve them of their undead status and Vlad had only intervened when she had turned her attention on the dog.

"She was ruthless."

"As was the Count."

"Quite."

"I'm not surprised that Martha decided to stay in the village and run the shop."

We all had mixed feelings about Martha remaining in the village, or rather a sense of impending doom, but it had been agreed that as long as she didn't cause trouble, we should leave her to get on with her life.

"Vlad and Mina seem well matched," Aunt Euphemia said. "I hope they are happy."

This was met with murmurs of agreement and as we returned to admiring the painting, and debating upon which wall it could be hung, Aunt Loveday returned. Cheeks flushed, white hair windblown, wearing Uncle Raif's oversized walking jacket and a pair of wellingtons, she was a little breathless, but her eyes glittered. We all turned to her as she stood in the open doorway.

"He's here!" she said. "I knew it this morning. I woke early to the moonlight and when thoughts of him filled my head, I knew it was time."

My aunts responded with a communal 'Ooh!'. Once again, I felt like a spectator in their conversation and could only imagine that she was talking about Eric, the Viking warrior who had died in her arms centuries ago but who she had recently been reunited with during our visit to the other realm.

"So," I ventured. "Are you going back there?"

"Don't be silly," Aunt Beatrice chided. "It's not Eric she's talking about."

I threw my aunt a look and shook my head; she was reading my thoughts again. "Then who?"

Aunt Loveday stepped into the kitchen and I noticed that she was carrying something hidden within the large coat.

"Him!" she said and pulled back the jacket to reveal a huge pair of eyes.

"Oh, he's gorgeous!"

"Beautiful!"

"Stunning!"

Enveloped by the coat was a large puppy with ears that flopped over huge and soulful brown eyes.

"A puppy! He's gorgeous," I enthused. "I had no idea you wanted one."

"I didn't, but it was his time to come, so I accepted."

Her words struck me as odd. "Did you just find him then?"

"No, he found me."

I stroked his soft fur and was rewarded by a lick. "He's beautiful," I said, enamoured.

The dog chuckled. "Thank you, kind lady!" The voice was deep and manly, and completely incongruous to the fluffy puppy with its floppy ears snuggled in Aunt Loveday's arms.

I withdrew my hand as though scalded.

Aunt Thomasin tittered behind me.

"Pray, do not stop. I find being stroked delightful."

This was no ordinary puppy, and I asked the obvious question. "Aunt Loveday, is this your new familiar?"

"Yes, it has been such a long time since my last." She sighed and sadness flickered in her eyes. "When Aethelstan passed, I was broken," she explained, "and could not countenance another companion, but over these last weeks, Renweard has been calling to me and this morning I knew it was time to bring him home."

"I am at your service, my lady," Renweard said.

Watching the puppy and listening to it speak in its old-fashioned way, was bizarre. I have to admit, I found it more than a little strange.

"I thank you," Aunt Loveday returned with courtesy.

"Renweard. Such a long time since I heard that name," Aunt Beatrice said.

"It means defender of the house."

"Perfect."

"It is, although I didn't choose his name, that is his given name."

I was intrigued and wanted to know more about the familiar process. Where did they come from? How were they chosen for us? Why did they come in different forms? And - with Lucifer in mind - could they be exchanged if they became too sour?

I gave him another stroke, marvelled at how soft his fur was, then, noticing how large his paws were, became curious of his breed. "So," I said, holding a large paw in my hand, not sure whether I should address Renweard, or Aunt Loveday, "what kind of dog will he grow up to be."

"Oh, I am sure he will be loyal and helpful," Aunt Loveday replied.

"That is my duty," Renweard agreed.

"No, I mean what breed of dog is he. What type? He's quite large for a puppy."

"Why, he's a wolfhound, of course. My familiars are always wolfhounds, Livitha. Just as yours are always cats. Our familiars may change over the centuries, but their form is always the same."

My aunts nodded in agreement.

Fascinated, I gave the pup a final stroke as Aunt Loveday set him down on the floor. He shook out his rough coat then sat by her feet as though to attention.

"Oh, he is going to be perfect," Aunt Beatrice enthused. "So calm!"

"Don't wolfhounds grow quite large?" I ventured.

"Oh, yes! They can grow quite enormous," Aunt Loveday explained, "but once Aethelstan grew through his puppyhood, he was quite manageable."

Aunt Thomasin groaned. "I had quite forgotten about that. It was chaos, Loveday."

"Well, puppies can be boisterous, but thankfully Renweard will grow to adulthood quite quickly."

Renweard raised a back leg and scratched his ear. He was adorable. "Do we take him for walks, like a normal dog?"

Renweard shook his head and was about to speak when a loud crack from the chimney breast brought our conversation to a halt.

Turning to the fireplace soot covered lumps fell into the hearth from inside the chimney.

Renweard growled.

As we exchanged glances, and Aunt Loveday stooped to re-assure the puppy, a shower of stone particles sprinkling onto the hearth was followed by a loud crack and a large split appeared at the centre of the stone mantel. Although the cottage was centuries old, my aunts magick kept it in good repair. Aunt Loveday placed her palm over the crack, muttering ancient words, but when she removed her hand the crack remained.

Loveday turned to face us. "Sisters," she said in a sombre tone, "Haligern is under attack!"

THE END

DEAR WITCHY MYSTERY fan!

'Menopause, Moon Magic, & Cursed Kisses' is the next book in the series and will be available very soon.

To receive an email straight to your inbox on publication day with a link to the book on Amazon in both ebook and paperback form, please sign up to my reader group. You can join via my website, or Facebook. Once you join please download my gift to you. Click here to join[1]

Website: www.jcblake.com[2]
Facebook: www.facebook.com/jcblakeauthor[3]

---

1.   https://dl.bookfunnel.com/pgh4acj6f8

2. http://www.jcblake.com

Other Books by the Author

If you love your mysteries with a touch of the supernatural then join ghost hunting team Peter Marshall, Meredith Blaylock, & Frankie D'Angelo in:

Marshall & Blaylock Investigations
When the Dead Weep[4]
Where Dead Men Hide[5]

Menopause, Magick, & Mystery
Hormones, Hexes, & Exes[6]
Hot Flashes, Sorcery, & Soulmates[7]
Night Sweats, Necromancy, & Love Bites
Menopause, Moon Magic, & Cursed Kisses

---

3. http://www.facebook.com/jcblakeauthor

4. https://books2read.com/u/bwdyA0

5. https://books2read.com/u/3GdV7L

6. https://books2read.com/u/4A7pJe

7. https://books2read.com/u/baaXg2

Printed in Great Britain
by Amazon